PRAISE FOR

This is a beautifully written story that sensitively evokes the rawness of grief and how it can trap the living – and if it doesn't make you cry, you must have a heart of flint.
DAILY MAIL

[A] touching temporal romance.
FINANCIAL TIMES

. . . this book stands out as a wonderful introduction for a new generation to discover the facts about the carnage and cruelty but also the humanity and courage which so marks these terrible events.
SCHOOL LIBRARIAN

Such is the strength and compassion in the writing that this is not a miserable read but an inspiration . . . Highly recommended.
HISTORICAL NOVEL SOCIETY

A moving exploration of the war's impact resonating down the years.
TONY BRADMAN, AUTHOR

. . . this heartbreaking story is essential reading for readers of all ages . . . There is a lot of emotion, romance, history and tragedy packed into the 150 pages . . .
SOUTH CHINA MORNING POST

A thought-provoking, original and deeply moving story which brings the war vividly to life.
JULIA ECCLESHARE

It's a short read but one that has a strong impact and stays in your head even after you've finished, ensuring that Valentine Joe's very real story will never be forgotten . . .
WONDROUS READS BLOG

I still have my uncle's ARP (Air Raid Precautions) badge. He was a warden during the Blitz and told me hair-raising stories of terror and courage set at a time when bombs fell on ordinary folk in London. But he had other stories, too: funny and dangerous tales of kids and animals allowed to play on bomb sites free from adult supervision!

Rebecca Stevens gets to the heart of both the bad parts and the good – and imagines what would happen if a girl from today went back to try and put past mistakes right. It's a very human story, and you'll love putting yourself in the shoes of a past generation. I suppose what's important to imagine is if we could pull together like they did – I think we would.

BARRY CUNNINGHAM
Publisher
Chicken House

Rose in the Blitz

Rebecca Stevens

Chicken House

2 Palmer Street, Frome, Somerset BA11 1DS
chickenhousebooks.com

Text © Rebecca Stevens 2016
First published in Great Britain in 2016
Chicken House
2 Palmer Street
Frome, Somerset BA11 1DS
United Kingdom
www.chickenhousebooks.com

Rebecca Stevens has asserted her right under the Copyright, Designs and
Patents Act 1988 to be identified as the author of this work.

Cover design and interior design by Helen Crawford-White
Cover photographs:
girl © Mark Owen/Trevillion Images
dog © Wisiel/Shutterstock
skyline © Everett Historical/ Shutterstock
Typeset by Dorchester Typesetting Group Ltd
Printed and bound in Great Britain by CPI Group (UK) Ltd, Croydon CR0 4YY

The paper used in this Chicken House book is made from
wood grown in sustainable forests.

1 3 5 7 9 10 8 6 4 2

British Library Cataloguing in Publication data available.

ISBN 978-1-910655-54-2
eISBN 978-1-910655-55-9

In memory of my mum and dad, Rosemary and John Stevens, and the men, women and children of all nations who died in the Second World War.

There's rosemary, that's for remembrance.
Pray you, love, remember.

Hamlet, William Shakespeare

1

'Rose? What's going on?'

Rose could see why her aunt was anxious. There were police officers everywhere. Some were on the move, slamming car doors and talking into their radios; others were standing around in clusters in their bright yellow jackets, drinking tea out of paper cups. Their cars were lined up along the side of the road, blue lights flashing, with two fire engines and an official-looking white van with a yellow stripe. A few passers-by were hanging about, looking as if they hoped something interesting was going to happen, and a little boy and his dad had stopped to admire the fire engines.

It was Mum who'd suggested they went out for a cup of tea. Tommy-dog could do with a walk, she'd said, and Aunt Cosy might like a breath of fresh air. Rose knew Mum just wanted them out of the way so she could prepare for the evening, but she didn't mind. She'd rather be out of the house anyway.

'What are all these policemen doing?' said Aunt Cosy.

1

'And why is there a soldier over there?'

She was right. A young soldier in British Army green was clambering out of the white van, adjusting his beret and joking with someone inside.

'I don't know, Aunt Cosy,' said Rose. 'I'll find out.'

The nearest police officer was a big man with a shiny pink face who was fussing about with a roll of blue-and-white plastic tape that read POLICE LINE DO NOT CROSS.

'They've found a bomb,' he said, without looking up.

Rose suddenly felt cold in spite of the May sunshine.

'A bomb?' she repeated.

The officer started wrapping his tape around the trunk of a huge tree that stood next to the old brick shelter at the corner of the common (which is what they called the area of open parkland near their house). Rose's grandad had told her the shelter was built during the last war and had tunnels that stretched for hundreds of metres, deep beneath those of the tube station opposite.

'Left over from World War Two,' said the officer. 'Unexploded. Builders found it buried under the grass while they were doing repairs on the bandstand.'

'But that's where we're going, isn't it, Rose?' Aunt Cosy looked so tiny, standing there with Tommy, very upright in her bright red jacket. 'The bandstand?'

'Not really, Aunt Cosy. We were going to go to the cafe. It's next to the bandstand. Remember?'

Rose felt bad as soon as she said it – the word 'remember'. Aunt Cosy hadn't been very good at remembering for a few years now, and it had got worse recently. Mum thought they should talk to a doctor, but Rose didn't see the point. Aunt Cosy was ninety-two, for goodness' sake. Ninety-two! Everyone gets a bit forgetful when they're that old, don't they?

The old lady had turned her smile on the police officer.

2

'I'm meeting somebody at the bandstand,' she told him. 'Somebody rather special.' They weren't meeting anybody, but Rose didn't say so. 'So you see, officer, it is rather important we get there on time.'

'I'm afraid that won't be possible, madam,' said the officer, straightening up and suddenly becoming more formal. 'The entire park has been evacuated.'

'Oh dear! Has it really? How long will we have to wait?'

'Until the bomb squad gives us the all-clear.' The officer trailed his tape across the path and wound it around another tree. 'Nice dog,' he added. Tommy wagged his tail. He didn't understand everything people said, but 'dog' was a word he recognised. 'What is he?'

'We're not sure,' said Rose. 'Part Jack Russell terrier, part springer spaniel, we think.'

The police officer made a big deal of looking at Tommy, who wagged his tail again, hoping he might produce some delicious treat from his pocket and give it to him as a reward for being a Good Dog.

'Nah,' he said. 'He's never got any springer in him. More like a bit of your Welsh collie. Rescue, was he?'

Rose nodded. 'Sort of,' she said. 'He was a stray.' She clipped the lead on to Tommy's collar. 'I suppose we'd best get back. Aunt Cosy?'

But Aunt Cosy had found another police officer to chat to, a woman this time, so Rose wandered over to a bench with Tommy and sat down. It was a perfect spring afternoon, the kind of day when sunshine shimmered through the petrol fumes and office workers lazed away their lunch hours on pavements outside pubs. A single plane floated silently past, leaving a trail of white vapour like a chalk mark across the blue blackboard of the sky. Rose wished she was on it, going somewhere else. France.

3

Germany. America maybe. China! Anywhere but here . . .

It was three years now since Dad had died and Mum needed to move on with her life. That's what her friends said anyway, the ones who came round to sit at the kitchen table and drink wine late into the night. Rose would hear them, after she'd gone to bed, murmuring together and laughing. And Mum *had* moved on now. She'd met Sal. His full name was Salvatore and he was Italian, a photographer, with a big, loud laugh and hairy arms and a son called Leo who was in year eight at school and thought he was funny but wasn't.

And Sal and Mum were getting married tomorrow.

Rose was glad Mum had been able to move on, she really was. It was just that *she* couldn't. She couldn't close a door on that part of her life, the part with Dad in it, not yet. And ever since Mum had told her about the wedding and how Sal and Leo were going to move into Aunt Cosy's house with them, she'd felt sort of empty – hollow, like a Russian doll with nothing inside.

She hadn't wanted to tell anyone how she felt, so had just carried on as if nothing had changed. And it hadn't, not really. School was OK, even though there were exams coming up. It was just . . . she wasn't particularly interested in it any more, even the subjects she used to love, like English and Psychology.

And it wasn't just school. Whenever her friends Grace and Ella suggested doing something, she never seemed to feel like it. She'd rather sit in her room with Tommy and stare out of the window or chat online with her friend Fred (they'd met a couple of years ago and even though they'd not seen each other again, had been messaging ever since). He lived in Germany so he wasn't going to suggest they meet up and go for a coffee or anything. But recently, as the wedding day got closer, she'd even

4

stopped chatting to him. She didn't know why, but when Fred wrote *Hey Rose, how are you?* she couldn't bring herself to reply.

What she wanted to write was: *Awful, actually. I feel horrible because my mum's getting married to a man with hairy arms who isn't my dad and they're going to live happily ever after and might even have a baby together and there'll be no room for me and I'll be left out and lonely for ever and ever . . .*

But she couldn't put that in a message. So she didn't write anything.

'Rose?' Aunt Cosy's face was sparkling with amusement. 'This young lady tells me she's found a bomb!'

'Yes, Aunt Cosy, I know—'

'I think it was very clever of her, but it does mean we can't get our cup of tea.'

'Then we'd better go home. D'you think?'

'I do think!' said Aunt Cosy. 'I do!'

'Come on, then. Tom?' Rose tugged his lead.

Tommy didn't move. He was standing quite still, listening with every part of his body.

'What's up?'

Aunt Cosy put her hand on Rose's arm. 'She's listening, darling.' For some reason, Aunt Cosy thought Tommy was a female dog called Sophie. Rose had given up trying to tell her otherwise. 'Dogs always hear them first,' she added.

'Hear what, Aunt Cosy?'

'Shh!' Her aunt was nodding as if greeting an old friend. 'The air raid sirens,' she said. 'They start at the edge of the city. Then they come towards you, whooshing in like waves, closer, closer, closer. Listen. That's our one now.'

Rose could hear . . . birdsong . . . the crackle and chat-

5

ter of the police radios . . . traffic . . . the usual cheerful roar of London. Nothing else.

'I can't—'

'Shh!' Aunt Cosy held up one finger and looked at the sky. A single bird crossed the blue. 'Where *are* you? Where *are* you? Where *are* you?' She repeated the words like a chant.

Rose was scared. Her aunt could be a bit strange sometimes, but she'd never seen her like this. 'What do you mean, Aunt Cosy?'

'It's the sound of the engines. I always think that's what they're saying: "Where are you?"'

'Engines?'

'The planes, darling. The German bombers.' The old lady grabbed Rose's arm. 'We must get to the shelter! It's starting, Rose! It's all starting again!'

2

By the time they got home, Aunt Cosy seemed to have forgotten about the planes and the air raid sirens. It was like that with memory loss, Mum said (she'd been reading about it and had become quite an expert). Sometimes you were completely fine. Other times, like when something unusual happened or you were in an unfamiliar place, you got – well – a bit forgetful.

'A bit forgetful?' Rose had repeated. 'Mum! She sees things that aren't there!'

'So do you,' Mum had replied, looking at her over her glasses. Rose couldn't argue with that. Dad always used to say she was like a satellite dish, picking up stuff that was floating around in the air, stuff that nobody else could see.

Aunt Cosy sat down with Mum in the kitchen to have the cup of tea she'd missed in the cafe, while Rose went up to her room with Tommy to check her phone.

There was a message from Fred. Just one word: *Rose?*

Rose knew he was wondering why she'd gone quiet on

him. But she couldn't reply. She didn't know what to say, didn't feel able to pretend that everything was all right when it wasn't. And she couldn't tell him how she was feeling, that would just be too weird. Maybe after the wedding she'd feel like it. Maybe after the wedding she'd feel better.

Maybe.

She looked at the dress hanging on the back of the door. It was a soft purpley-blue colour, plain cotton, knee-length with a full skirt and long sleeves. She hadn't wanted anything too fancy. Neither had Mum. Her dress was silk, a darker shade of the same colour, and Aunt Cosy's was even darker, a deep shade of violet, so dark it was almost black. She'd bought a hat as well, with grey silk flowers that matched her hair, and a long black feather. The old lady loved dressing up and had been looking forward to the wedding for ages.

Unlike Rose. She was going to be Mum's bridesmaid and she was dreading it.

She touched the dress, feeling its softness between her finger and thumb, then sat down on the bed with Tommy curled up in his usual place at the end. The room was beginning to get dark as the daylight faded outside the window but she didn't turn on the light. She liked this time of day when the air turned grey and grainy with dusk and the room filled up with shadows.

Rose had wanted this room, even though it was smaller than the other bedrooms, because it was at the back of the house and looked out over the garden. They'd been living here nearly a year now, she and Mum, in the house on Nightingale Lane. Neither of them had wanted to stay in the old house in Balham where every chip on the paintwork, every creak of the floorboards reminded them of Dad. So when Mum's ninety-two-year-old relative had suggested they move in with her, it seemed the perfect solution.

Aunt Cosy wasn't really an aunt; she was the cousin of Mum's grandmother, which made her Rose's cousin twice removed (or something equally difficult to remember). She'd never had children of her own, but had always been a very special person in Mum's life, a sort of extra grandma, and was actually the reason why Rose was called Rose. Aunt Cosy's real name was Rosemary, though she'd always been known as Cosy in the family. It was something to do with a little sister who couldn't say Rosemary properly and the name had stuck.

Mum said she'd always loved coming to her Aunt Cosy's house when she was little and Rose felt the same. It seemed so big and old and mysterious, full of shadowy corners and things to discover. There was a stuffed owl in the living room and a cuckoo clock from Germany in the hall, made of carved black wood. It didn't keep very good time (in other words, Dad said, it was always wrong), and the cuckoo seemed to come out of its little door at random and cuckoo as many times as it liked. Once Rose had counted thirteen *cuck*s and twelve *oo*s (the last *cuck* was left hanging in the air without an *oo*, leaving Rose with a strange, unsatisfied feeling). The bird often seemed to emerge whenever she walked past and she suspected it of watching from behind its door so it could pop out especially to make her jump.

And then there was the overgrown garden with its birdbath and stone frog hidden in the grass, and the funny old shed that wasn't really a shed at all but something called an Anderson shelter. Everybody had them in their gardens in the war, Aunt Cosy said, you'd go out and sleep there to be safe from the bombs (though Rose didn't understand why you'd be safer in a rickety-looking

9

shed than a nice solid house). The shelter was half buried in the ground with grass and weeds sprouting from the roof, which made it look as if it had grown out of the earth, and whenever Rose and her parents had come to visit (which they used to do nearly every Sunday) she'd leave the grown-ups drinking tea in the kitchen and make her way down the garden to go inside.

The house must be worth a fortune now, Mum said, being so near the common, but Aunt Cosy would never sell it. She'd lived there all her life and it was too full of memories. It was funny, Rose thought, that she and Mum had left their little house in Balham to get away from their memories and now they were living in the middle of someone else's.

Her phone buzzed on the bed. Fred again? No, Grace. *OK for tomorrow?!!!!!!!*

No, thought Rose, *I'm not OK. I'll never be OK. Not in a million years will I ever be OK.*

She turned off her phone and felt in the pocket of her parka, remembering the invitation that Mum had asked her to take to school for Grace. She'd forgotten all about it, but it didn't matter, Grace was coming anyway. Rose opened the envelope and pulled out the stiff white card.

WE'RE GETTING MARRIED!

it announced in curly gold writing.

Please join Elizabeth, Sal,
Rose, Leo, Rosemary and Tommy
at 2.00 p.m. on 11th May 2016
at the Windmill Inn, Clapham Common
to celebrate our wedding!

She shoved it back in her pocket, not wanting Mum to find out she'd forgotten it, then went over to the window and stared out into the thickening dusk. The guests would be arriving soon, and she'd have to go down and get kissed to death by all of Sal's relations who'd come over from Italy for the wedding. Still, Grandad would be there and that would make it more OK.

She opened the window, heaving up the sash and leaning out with her elbows on the sill. The air was still warm and smelled of wet leaves and damp earth. Tommy plopped off the bed and padded across the room to stand next to her. She could feel his warm weight against her leg as she listened to the hum of the city outside.

'*I know where I'm going and I know who's going with me . . .*'

It was the girl next door. Rose had never actually seen her but she often heard her singing at this time of the evening, when Mum had come in from work and was clattering about in the kitchen. It was always the same song, simple and sweet, the melody curling up through the dusk.

'*I know who I love, but I don't know who I'll marry . . .*'

As the voice faded away, Tommy pricked up his ears as he heard the knock at the front door. The guests had started to arrive.

Rose sighed and looked at her face in the mirror. Time to go down.

'All right, Cabbage?' Grandad kissed Rose on the forehead and ruffled Tommy's fur. 'And how's my favourite dog?'

Tommy was wagging his tail so hard that his whole body wagged with it, and sneezing with excitement. He and Grandad had a special relationship. Not as special as the one between him and Rose, but still special.

'How you feeling about tomorrow?' Grandad said, looking at Rose over his glasses.

Rose nodded. 'Yeah,' she said. 'OK. Fine. Looking forward to it.'

Grandad knew that wasn't true and Rose knew that he knew it wasn't true, but they both pretended it was.

'And how's that handsome pen pal of yours?'

'What pen pal?' Rose knew who Grandad was talking about, but she wasn't going to admit it.

'German boy. You know. What's-his-name, Fred.'

'He is not a pen pal, Grandad.'

'You write to each other, don't you?'

'No. Well, yes. But not with pens. We message.'

'Message.' Grandad didn't like it when people used words in new ways. 'A message is a noun, Rose, not a verb.'

'You know what I mean, Brian.' When Rose was little she'd heard her grandma calling Grandad by his first name and had copied her. Now she always did it when she wanted to make a point. 'Don't pretend to be even older than you are.'

He laughed and Rose felt better. Tommy wagged his tail again, watching them both.

'Anyway, Fred is definitely not a pen pal,' she said. 'You need pens to be pen pals.'

'What is he, then?' said Grandad.

'I don't know. A friend. Someone I know. Why does he have to be anything?'

Grandad shrugged, then sucked his teeth. They both looked across the room to where Mum had left her own mum and dad by the food and was now talking to Sal's parents. They didn't speak much English and Mum was gesturing wildly to try and make herself understood. Sal

12

was watching her performance and laughing, refusing to help. Rose wondered how such a neat, timid-looking couple had produced this big, untidy man with the loud laugh and crumbs in his beard. Families were weird.

Everyone seemed to have made an effort to dress up for the party. Mum had bought a new top in dark-red silk and even Sal had swapped his usual checked shirt for what looked like a fresh new white one. Aunt Cosy looked lovely, Rose thought, in the embroidered Chinese jacket she always brought out for special occasions. It was black silk, covered in birds and flowers and dragons in red and gold and green.

Rose looked down at her black jeans and boots. Maybe she should have got changed. She knew Mum would have liked her to make more of an effort. There hadn't been a lot of time though, after she and Aunt Cosy had got back from the common. Plus she didn't have anything to wear, not really. And Leo had been hogging the bathroom, as usual . . .

Now Leo was over by the food, eating crisps and trying to squirm away from his Italian grandmother who had escaped from Mum and was pinching his cheek. *My stepbrother*, Rose thought. *He's going to be my stepbrother.* It didn't seem possible. She couldn't imagine him as anything other than an annoying thirteen-year-old boy who left the toilet seat up and made jokes that no one else thought were funny.

This was what it was going to be like from now on. Mum and Sal making each other laugh, and Leo hogging the bathroom. And Rose on her own, hiding in her bedroom, not talking to anyone.

'Rose?' Grandad was staring into his drink as if he'd discovered something very interesting at the bottom of the glass. 'There's something I should tell you.'

'What is it, Brian?'

Grandad harrumphed and shuffled his feet, then looked across the room as if he hoped someone would come and rescue him. Mum had put some music on and Aunt Cosy was waltzing with Sal's father. 'I've done something I probably shouldn't have . . .'

'What d'you mean?'

Grandad took a deep breath, then looked her in the eye. 'Your young man—' He stopped. 'Sorry. Fred, I mean. I know he's not your young man . . .'

'What about him?' Rose felt a sudden panic rising in her chest. 'Grandad? What have you done?'

'I invited him to the wedding tomorrow.' The words came out in a rush.

Rose couldn't speak. The room seemed to swoop and rock around her. She could still hear the voices and the music but they seemed to be coming from a long way away. *He can't . . . I can't . . . it's too . . .*

She didn't know what to do. She didn't know what she was feeling. She just knew she didn't want Fred to come to the wedding.

'I realise now I shouldn't have.' She became aware of Grandad's voice again. 'Not without asking you first. Your mum said—'

'So why did you?'

Rose hadn't realised how loudly she'd spoken until she noticed that the people near them had stopped talking and were looking at her from the corners of their eyes. But she was too upset to care. A hot wave of misery rose up from her chest, making her cheeks burn and her eyes sting and the words tumble out of her mouth.

'How could you, Grandad?' She was nearly shouting now. 'It's none of your – none of your—'

'I know, I know.' Grandad rubbed his face. 'I'm sorry.

14

I just thought—'

'What? What did you think? That it would be a lovely surprise for me?'

'I suppose so. It was stupid. I see that now. I'm really sorry, Cabbage—'

'No!' Rose felt her eyes brimming with angry tears. 'It's too late! Why does everyone keep trying to do things for me? Why do they think they know what I want? This is hard enough for me anyway, all this – this . . .' She gestured at the room. The music was still playing but Aunt Cosy and Sal's dad had stopped dancing and Mum's parents were exchanging worried looks. Everyone was trying to pretend nothing was happening, trying to pretend they weren't listening. Rose knew they were, but she was too upset to stop. 'And now you've made it a million times worse!'

'Rose—' Mum had come over. Her hand was on Grandad's arm.

'No!' Rose was crying now. 'You can't make it better! It's too late! It's too late for anything!'

'Rose, sweetheart,' said Mum. 'Wait—'

But she had gone.

3

Rose stumbled through the hall, where the cuckoo clock was clearing its throat in preparation to strike, and went into the kitchen, with Tommy following on behind. The sink was already filling up with dirty plates and empty bottles and the back door was open, letting the blue-black night spread like ink into the bright muddle of the house. She couldn't bear being indoors any more, not with everyone looking at her, all concerned and interested, so she stepped out into the cool scented dampness of the garden and made her way along the slippery path to the Anderson shelter.

It was totally dark inside, but she wasn't scared. Nothing really bad could happen when Tommy was around. She felt for the old hurricane lamp they kept on the ledge inside the door. It cast a pale cold light over the friendly clutter of flowerpots, empty paint tins and old garden tools that filled the shelter. Rose sat down on the bench that ran along one side and got out her phone.

My grandad just told me he invited you tomorrow don't

expect you were planning to come anyway but please don't he shouldn't have invited you sorry for misunderstanding bye

No names, no kisses, no stupid emoticons.

She read it though twice and then she pressed send. A tear splodged on the screen. Surely Fred wouldn't come now?

'Rose?'

The door of the shed was ajar and a small figure was visible in the darkness outside. Rose quickly wiped her eyes with the back of her hand.

'May I come in?'

It was Aunt Cosy. The door made its horrible scraping noise on the path as she pulled it open and made her careful way down the steps. Tommy stood up politely and wagged his tail as she came over and sat down on the bench next to Rose. Neither of them said anything for a minute. Then:

'You all right, Strange Girl?' Aunt Cosy had called her that sometimes ever since she was little. Rose never knew why, but she liked it. It made her feel special, as if she and the old lady shared some mysterious secret.

'Am I all right about what?' Rose knew she sounded a bit rude but she couldn't help it.

'Your mum getting married.'

Rose stared down at her fingernails. Tommy had started rootling about among some flowerpots. She hoped he wasn't going to wee on them.

Aunt Cosy tapped the back of Rose's hand three times with her forefinger. Her hand sparkled with rings. 'He's a nice man, you know, Rose.'

'I know.' Rose couldn't stop herself sounding impatient.

'And he loves your mum very much.'

'Aunt Cosy – you don't have to tell me—'

17

'Ah, but I do. Rose. Look at me.' The old lady's eyes were a dark shiny brown, almost black, like buttons. When Rose was little she used to call them Aunt Cosy's mouse eyes. 'She loves him too, Rose.'

'I know that!' Rose knew she was being unreasonable, selfish even, but she couldn't help it. She didn't need people to keep reminding her how much her mum loved this man who wasn't her dad. 'I can't help how I feel, though.'

'No,' her aunt said. 'You can't. But you can talk about it. You can tell me. I know that won't make it go away but it might help a little bit.'

'OK!' Rose felt her cheeks getting hot as the words bubbled up. 'I hate it, if you want to know. I really really hate it. I don't want to share my mum with someone who's not my dad. I don't want them living here.' She turned and looked her aunt full in the face. 'Do *you* want them living here, Aunt Cosy?'

'It's a big house. I like company. Why not?'

'Yes, but . . .' Rose felt the anger drain away and tears prick in her eyes. 'I don't much like Sal, Aunt Cosy. He tries too hard to be nice. And he smells weird.' Sal didn't really smell weird, Rose knew that. He probably smelt quite nice to most people – of woolly jumpers and coffee and the stuff he put on his beard. He just didn't smell like Dad.

'Does he?' Aunt Cosy seemed genuinely interested. 'I've never noticed. I'll have to give him a good old sniff when we go in.' She gave a little snort of laughter and tapped Rose's hand again. 'I do understand, you know,' she said. 'I lost someone special when I was about your age.'

'In the war?'

Aunt Cosy nodded. She stared at nothing for a

18

moment, then turned back to Rose. 'So that is why, sweetheart, your mum is right to grab this new love with both hands and hang on to it for dear life.'

'But . . .' The shed swam in front of Rose's eyes. 'I'm scared, Aunt Cosy.' The words tumbled out of her mouth before she could stop them.

'Of what, dear heart?'

She was scared there'd be no place for her in the shiny new life her mum was making with her new husband. She was scared that if she got closer to Fred, she'd start needing him and then he'd disappear, just like everyone else. But she couldn't say that. So she didn't say anything.

'Is it this boy your grandad's been telling me about? The one from Germany who seems to like you so much?'

'No!' The word came out too quickly and Rose saw Aunt Cosy hide a tiny smile.

'Have a feel under the bench, would you, sweet? There's something I want to show you.'

Rose crouched down and felt about in the gritty dampness. She hoped there were no slugs. Or earwigs. She hated them the most with their pincers and their horrible shiny scuttle.

'I can't feel – oh.'

There was something.

Rose needed both hands to pull the old tin box from under the bench. It was rusty and covered with dirt and crumbs of concrete which she brushed off with one hand, revealing a design of flowers and birds on a faded blue background. There were no earwigs.

'What is it?' Rose put it on the bench between them.

'Memories.' Her aunt traced the outline of a faded pink rose on the lid with one finger. 'You might have noticed, Rose dear, that I've recently become a rather old

19

woman. So old I can't remember how old I am.'

'You're ninety-three next birthday.' As soon as the words were out of her mouth, Rose wondered if she should have lied.

'Ninety-three? Goodness! That's even older than I thought. Are you sure?'

Rose nodded.

'Ah well, if you say so, it must be true.' She shook her head. 'Whoever would have thought it? Ninety-three! When I was your age, none of us thought we'd make it into our twenties.'

'Because of the war?'

She nodded. 'You couldn't take anything for granted, it would have felt like bad luck. Not that we thought about it all the time. It was just there, at the back of our minds, like a sort of hum: will I make it, will I make it, will I make it through another night?'

'Was it like that all through the war?'

'In the Blitz it was, when we were being bombed every night. People didn't just say "goodnight" at the end of the day. They said "goodnight, good luck". It became quite normal, you see, to think you might not be around in the morning.' She sat for a minute, lost in the memory.

What must it have been like, thought Rose, *to know that every night might be your last?*

'But it was exciting, in a way.' Aunt Cosy seemed to guess what Rose was thinking. 'Made you want to make the most of every moment you had. Try and keep hold of every single one of them, hang it in your memory like a charm on a bracelet.' She patted Rose's hand again. 'But now my moments are starting to trickle away. Which is why I want to share them with you.'

Rose was surprised to feel her eyes prickle with more tears. She blinked them away quickly.

'Look.' Her aunt had opened the box and was holding a photograph, black and white, mounted on stiff card. It was of a young woman, a girl of about Rose's age but dressed as if she was much older. She was wearing dark lipstick and a pale lady-like blouse with a bow at the neck. Her hair was dark, neatly curled and perfect-looking as if she'd just come from the hairdresser. But her dark eyes sparkled with mischief as they looked out of the photograph and her mouth seemed to be twitching at the corners as if she was trying not to laugh.

She looks a bit like me, Rose thought. Of course, she'd never do her hair like that or wear that dark-red lipstick but apart from that . . . And then she realised. 'It's you! Isn't it, Aunt Cosy? It's you, when you were young!'

Her aunt shook her head at the girl in the picture as if she was a naughty child. 'Look at her,' she said. 'All done-up to the nines. The hair! My mother lent me that blouse,' she added. 'It was a particularly nasty shade of mint green.'

Rose looked at her aunt and saw the young girl in the photo looking back at her from behind her eyes. It was as if the old lady's soft, lined face was just a mask with eyeholes that the young girl was looking through. Aunt Cosy sighed and turned back to the box.

'Let's see. What else have we got in our box of tricks?'

Rose felt around and brought out a lipstick in a tarnished gold case. When she opened it, it smelled of dust and wax.

'Is this the lipstick you're wearing in the photo?'

'I should think so. It would've been the only one I had. It was so hard to get hold of in the war, we treasured every scrap. And this . . .'

Her aunt was holding a gold signet ring between the thumb and forefinger of her right hand.

'Is it yours?' said Rose. 'It looks like a man's.' There was a little smile dancing round Aunt Cosy's lips that made Rose smile too. 'Aunt Cosy? Did someone give it to you?'

'One that got away, sweetheart. One that got away.'

The old lady looked in the box and brought out a newspaper cutting, fragile and yellow with age. There was a small, dark photograph of a young man in uniform, smiling at the camera, and a headline: COMMONWEALTH AIRMAN MISSING IN ACTION. The young man was black, very handsome and very young-looking, not much older than the boys Rose went to school with.

Her aunt seemed to know what she was thinking. 'He was nineteen,' she said and touched the boy's face with one crooked forefinger. 'His name was Johnny.'

'And – he never came back?'

'No,' she said. 'He never came back.' Then she began to sing:

'I know where I'm going and I know who's going with me
I know who I love, but I don't know who I'll marry
Some say he's bad, but I say he's bonny
The fairest of them all, my handsome, winsome Johnny.'

'What is that song?' Rose said, when the last notes had faded away. 'It's lovely. I hear her singing it nearly every night, the girl next door.'

Aunt Cosy shook her head. 'No, sweetheart, there's no girl next door. Just the couple with the cat on the one side, city boy on the other.'

'Then . . . who is it I hear singing?'

Aunt Cosy gave her one of her bright smiles. 'It's me, sweetheart,' she said. 'Shall we go in?'

4

Grandad was washing up when Rose and Aunt Cosy came in from the garden.

'Well, look who it is!' he said. 'The wanderers return!'

Aunt Cosy reached up and patted his cheek, then left the room without a word, probably so Rose and Grandad could be alone together. Rose took a deep breath. She knew she should apologise, say sorry for what happened earlier. Grandad was only trying to be nice, she knew that, and she felt bad for storming out. But she couldn't. She looked at him, standing at the sink wearing Dad's old apron, the one with blue and white stripes, and opened her mouth to speak. But nothing came out.

'All sorted now, Cabbage?'

He tried to smile, to pretend everything was all right. Rose's heart flipped, but she still couldn't say anything.

'Look, love . . .' Grandad shook the bubbles off his hands, dried them on his apron and took a step towards her. Rose could see the grey beard bristles on his chin and the little scar above his eye. 'About what happened earlier—'

And then Mum came in with a pile of dirty plates, so Rose slipped past her and headed up to her room.

It was late now and the last of the guests had gone some time ago. Rose checked her phone. Fred hadn't replied to her message, but then why should he? She'd made it pretty clear she didn't want him to come to the wedding, the invitation had been a mistake. She'd even implied she didn't want to see him at all. He'd probably never message her again.

Tommy looked up as he heard footsteps coming up the stairs. Mum and Sal were going to bed, but Rose didn't feel tired, so she went over to the window and looked out at the night. The moon was floating above the roofs, a perfect silver disc, and the garden was all navy-blue and silver in the moonlight. In the distance a fox answered the scream of a police car's siren with an unearthly screech. Rose shivered and thought about the bomb in the middle of the common, lying there beneath the earth for all those years, waiting for someone to find it. Waiting to explode.

Tommy's ears went up as there was a tap on the door.

'Rose?'

It was Aunt Cosy again. She was wearing her silky blue dressing gown and red velvet slippers, and the grey hair she usually wore up in a bun was hanging in a little plait down her back, which made her look younger and older at the same time.

'Just got up to go to the lav, sweetheart. Saw your light on under the door.' She came in and made her way over to the window. 'Why are you still up, Rose? We've got a big day tomorrow.'

'I know,' said Rose. 'I was just going to bed.'

They stood together in silence for a moment, then: 'She's there again, Rose.'

'The fox?'

There was a fox that visited their garden sometimes, perhaps the same one Rose had just heard. She and Aunt Cosy looked out for her and Rose occasionally left her a plate of Tommy's food. But she knew her aunt didn't mean the fox. Not this time.

'What can you see, Aunt Cosy? Tell me.'

But as she followed her aunt's gaze, she realised there was no need for the old lady to describe her vision. Because she could see it too.

The garden looked the same. The hump of the Anderson shelter, the straggly lilac tree in the corner. It was the sky that was different. It was exploding with silent fireworks, making the garden whirl with speckles of white light, as if the moon was a giant mirror ball and the whole world was a dance floor. And someone was dancing. Down in the garden, in the middle of the whirling lights, a little girl was dancing barefoot on the grass, holding up her hands to the sky and spinning in celebration of this unexpected firework display.

Rose realised she'd stopped breathing. *Who is she?* She didn't know if she'd said the words out loud or only thought them. She dragged her eyes away from the window and turned to her aunt. 'Aunt Cosy? Who's that little girl?'

But Aunt Cosy had gone.

'Aunt Cosy?'

She went to the door. The landing was empty. For a second Rose wondered if she'd dreamt the whole thing. And then she heard the front door slam. 'Aunt Cosy!'

There was no light beneath the door of Mum's room, and Rose couldn't bear to knock and disturb them (she

25

still couldn't get used to it being 'them' in there). No. She'd sort this out on her own. She ducked back into her room, grabbed her parka and her phone, and made for the stairs

'Rose?'

It was Leo, in his pyjamas, peering down the landing. He looked even younger than usual, with his hair tousled and his face all blurry with sleep.

'Go back to bed, Leo. It's fine. Everything's fine.' Rose struggled to make her voice sound normal.

'But—'

'Really!' Rose hadn't meant to sound so aggressive. 'Sorry. It's just Aunt Cosy wandering again. You go back to bed.'

Leo shrugged. 'If you say so.'

'I do.' Whatever was happening, Rose was going to deal with it on her own.

She hurried downstairs with Tommy behind her, his claws tapping on the wood. As they got to the hall, the cuckoo clock started the throat-clearing noise it always made before the cuckoo burst into action. But this time, nothing happened. It was as if the cuckoo had second thoughts about leaving his nest. Rose looked at the time. It was midnight. Tomorrow had become today, and today Mum was getting married.

'Come on, Tom.'

He wagged his tail as she opened the door, and shot out in front of her.

Nightingale Lane looked quite ordinary in the orange glow of the street lights. A young couple was walking home hand in hand, and a group of laughing girls stumbled along, trying to hail a taxi. A night bus rumbled past at the end of the street. But where was Aunt Cosy?

'Wuff!'

Tommy had spotted her, heading in the direction of the tube station, moving surprisingly fast for an old lady of nearly ninety-three.

'Come on, Tom!'

And so they ran, past the pub and the old school, past the low-level blocks of flats that Grandad said had been built to fill the spaces where houses were bombed in the war, past the old-fashioned flower shop with its metal shutters closed against the night, just in time to see Aunt Cosy disappearing into the dark entrance of the tube station. Why was it still open? It was too late for the trains to be running, wasn't it?

There was no time to think. With Tommy behind her, Rose followed her aunt into the station.

It had begun.

It was dark inside the ticket hall. The blue-black sky seemed to press down on the glass dome of the roof and there was a sour smell that reminded Rose of the breath of her least favourite Maths teacher. A page from an old newspaper stirred in one corner as Rose's footsteps echoed on the tiled floor, but there was no sign of Aunt Cosy. There was no sign of anyone. Rose felt in her pocket for her travel card, then realised there was no need – the barriers were open. Anyway, she told herself, she and Tommy weren't going to *go* anywhere. They were just going to look around the station and find Aunt Cosy before—

The thought hit Rose with a thud.

Before she gets on a train.

'Tommy! Quick!'

He was off, shooting through the barrier as if he was chasing a squirrel on the common. Rose ran after him and the escalator carried them down, past walls lined with identical adverts, announcing something called a 'memory walk'. A 'walk down memory lane', they said, to raise money to fight dementia. Dementia. Rose knew that was what Mum thought was wrong with Aunt Cosy, but she had no time to think of that now. As she and Tommy jumped over the last step, Rose heard the urgent rumble of an approaching train and felt its hot breath on her face with its familiar smell of dust and electricity. Which platform? Which way? *Which way?*

Tommy seemed to know. He headed to the left, the northbound platform. A train was already there, its doors open as if it was waiting for them. Rose checked the length of the platform, but there was no sign of Aunt Cosy. That meant one thing: *she must have got on the train.*

Rose had never been on the tube this late, not on her own, and she knew Mum would be furious if she did. But Tommy didn't hesitate. He hopped through the doors of the last carriage as if it was something he did every day. Rose followed just in time. The doors closed behind them, there was a self-important whirring sound as the engine geared up to leave, and the train lurched off into the darkness.

Rose stood, balancing herself against the movement of the train, and looked around. *It must be one of the oldest trains they had,* she thought, with its scratchy-looking upholstered seats and wobbly round things hanging down from the ceiling for you to grab on to when the carriage was full and you had to stand—

But this carriage wasn't full. *It was completely empty.*

Aunt Cosy had probably got on further along, Rose told herself. All she had to do was walk up the train and she'd find her. She pictured the old lady, sitting alone in a carriage near the front, smiling to herself as the train rattled along. Maybe humming that song of hers. Rose would sit down next to her and put her hand over her aunt's tiny knobbly one with all its glittering rings, and say, 'Where *are* you going, Aunt Cosy?' And Aunt Cosy would turn to her with a surprised smile and shake her head and admit that she didn't know. 'I'm a silly old woman,' she'd say and then she'd laugh and Tommy would wag his tail and Rose would say, 'I think we'd better go home now.' And everything would be all right.

So she started walking, swaying and lurching as the train rattled along, heaving open the doors between the carriages – stepping over the gaps that used to scare her so much when she was little, hoping that Aunt Cosy would be in the next one, the next one, the next one . . . And each time, her heart sinking as she realised that this carriage was empty too.

The last door was locked. They'd reached the front of the train, the driver's door. The train really was completely empty.

And there was something else.

Rose knew this route, knew it really well. She must have been on it a million times, heading north to go shopping in Oxford Street with Mum or west to a museum with Dad, so she knew that there were loads of stops on this line, one every few minutes. But this train just rattled on and on through the darkness, swinging round the bends as if it was in a hurry to get somewhere.

Perhaps it's the last train of the night, Rose thought. It was late, after all. They might end up at some depot and then she'd have to call Mum. She wouldn't be too pleased to be woken up in the middle of the night before her wedding, but she'd understand when Rose explained and told her she hadn't wanted to disturb her. It would be a relief to tell her in a way, to hear her voice on the phone,

29

a bit cross, but reassuringly normal and organised. Mum would come and get her, and then she'd phone the police, explain that an old lady had gone missing, and they'd find her really quickly, much quicker than Rose could on her own.

And then the train stopped, shuddering to a halt with a gasping sound.

Rose peered through the window, the glass cold against her nose. It was too dark to see much, but it didn't look as if they'd stopped in the middle of a tunnel, and when the doors opened, she could see there was a platform outside.

'Where are we?'

It didn't look like a station, not one that was in use anyway. Grandad had told Rose about these tube stations that had been abandoned for some reason and left empty and unchanged over the years, their old names still on the walls next to advertisements for brands of soap and cigarettes and sweets that you could no longer buy, while the trains rattled through without stopping. Ghost stations, he said they were called. Perhaps this was one of those.

Rose and Tommy looked at each other. The open doors of the train seemed to be waiting for them.

'Come on, Tom.'

As they stepped on to the platform, the doors slid shut behind them and the train pulled away. They were completely alone.

Rose felt a bubble of panic rising in her chest. She took out her phone. There was no signal down here, of course. She'd just have to find a way out, go up to ground level, call Mum from there. There had to be an emergency staircase or something, even if the escalators weren't working. Even if this was a ghost station. It was certainly much dirtier and darker than the ones she was used to and there was no sign, nothing to tell her where they were.

Just as the bubble of panic was about to burst, Rose felt the ground begin to tremble and a familiar blast of hot air stirred the clots of black dust on the ground. Another train was arriving. Not on this platform though, it must be a southbound train. One that would take them home then, back to Clapham South.

Tommy must have been thinking the same. Rose ran after him as he skittered away into a passageway leading off the platform. It was even darker here. The tiles on the wall were cracked and stained and great drifts of greasy-looking dust and rubbish moved in the corners like leaves on autumn pavements. And there was the station sign.

Clapham South.

They were back where they had started.

How was that possible? They couldn't have gone in a circle; this line went south to north, north to south. It had to be a mistake. Didn't it? *Didn't it?*

Rose heard the train doors whoosh open on the other platform and then, footsteps and bustle, the sounds of people getting off. A lot of people by the sound of it. *Why was the station suddenly so busy? Where had all these people come from in the middle of the night?*

And now they were upon them, hurrying through from the platform: men wearing hats and dark suits, with moustaches and briefcases; some were in uniform, soldiers by the look of it; and there were women too, in neat jackets and skirts, dark lipstick, and curled hair bouncing as they moved. But the strangest thing about them wasn't their clothes. It was something else.

They were all white.

The London Rose knew was full of all sorts of different types of people, people whose families had come from all over the world to settle there. It was partly what made it so interesting, so much fun to live there.

But all these people were white.

And as Rose watched them, pressed up against the station sign with Tommy beside her, a feeling of coldness crept over her as she realised there was no mistake. This was Clapham South station. It just wasn't the one she was familiar with.

What's happening? she thought. *What am I supposed to do? Where am I supposed to go?*

She followed the crowd. There was nothing else she could do. She stepped on to the escalator with Tommy beside her, gripping the moving handrail to stop herself shaking, and keeping her eyes fixed on the broad khaki back of the soldier in front of her. The escalator wasn't made of the familiar snaky metal, it was wooden, and it carried them from the gloomy depths at the bottom into bright sunshine. It had been past midnight when they'd left, but now the sky above the glass dome in the roof was bright blue and sunlight lit every corner of the ticket hall.

It wasn't just the station that had changed, it was the time of day.

Hands clenched in her pockets, Rose allowed herself to be swept past a uniformed guard, who was checking tickets in a half-hearted way, and out of the station where she stopped and looked around, blinking in the sun.

It was the same street but different, so different. The cars and taxis rumbling past were bigger, blacker, bulkier than she was used to and there were far fewer of them. The shops were dark and dingy-looking, some were boarded up. There were no flowers outside what Rose knew as the flower shop – it had nothing in the window but a white china dish containing some dull, chalky-looking sweets. A young boy was selling newspapers from a pile outside, while another smaller boy squatted nearby,

32

drawing lines for noughts and crosses on the pavement with a piece of chalk.

An elderly woman in a shapeless mud-coloured coat shook her head at Rose as she passed. 'Some people!' she muttered loud enough to make sure that she could hear. 'Don't they know there's no dogs allowed in the stations these days? Tuh!'

These days? thought Rose. *What are these days? Where am I?*

Across the road, the common looked reassuringly familiar, although there was no sign of the old brick shelter. And what were those huge silvery balloons that hung above the trees in the distance, looking like flabby floating elephants? Rose shivered. There was a chill in the air in spite of the sunshine, and the leaves of the great plane tree on the corner were beginning to turn. It was autumn, then, she thought. It had been spring when they left. So the season had changed as well . . .

And then she saw her. Standing under the tree like a ghost in the sunshine, a tiny upright figure in a silky blue dressing gown and red velvet slippers, looking straight at Rose. Aunt Cosy. So that was it.

Her aunt had gone for a walk down memory lane. And she'd taken Rose with her.

5

Rose didn't stop to think. She stepped into the road.

'Hey!'

Someone grabbed her arm, jerking her back. An old red double-decker bus roared past, horn blaring, the conductor standing on the platform at the back shouting at her. Rose turned and looked into the face of the person who'd saved her.

It was the young man in the photograph, Aunt Cosy's lost love.

Johnny.

He was actually there, standing in front of her, as large as life and twice as natural (as Grandad would say). He looked younger than he did in Aunt Cosy's photograph, and he wasn't in uniform. He was wearing a soft-looking white shirt open at the neck under an old grey jacket that looked as if it had once been part of a suit that belonged to someone else. And he was even more hand-some in real life, with eyes that looked at you as if he'd known you for ever and a mouth that seemed as if it was about to laugh.

Johnny.

'What is happening here?' he said. He had a warm voice with an accent of some sort, Rose didn't know what. It didn't sound African. Grace's dad was from Nigeria and it didn't sound like him. West Indian, maybe? Jamaican? 'You are *trying* to get yourself killed?'

Rose realised she was holding her breath. 'I'm sorry,' she said. 'I thought I saw someone I knew . . .'

She looked across the road. The bus had gone past now, but there was no sign of the small figure under the plane tree. Aunt Cosy had disappeared.

'I'm sorry,' she said again. 'I'll be more careful next time.'

Johnny shook his head. 'I think you should go home,' he said. 'It has been quiet so far but might not be so quiet tonight.'

And then he smiled.

It was a smile that made you feel like you were the most beautiful, interesting, funny person in the world, not someone who was often grumpy, sometimes got spots and was currently fed up because your mum was getting married to a man who wasn't your dad. It was the kind of smile that made you smile back.

So Rose did. She smiled back and Tommy wagged his tail, thumping it against her legs.

'Yes,' she said. 'I will. Thank you. Sorry.' And then, because he was about to go and she didn't want him to, 'Can I ask you something?'

She wanted to ask him if he'd met Aunt Cosy yet, tell him to be careful, not to join up, but she couldn't, of course she couldn't. He wouldn't understand. She didn't understand herself. So when she opened her mouth a different question came out.

'What's the date?'

'The date?'

He looked at her to see if she was joking, but when he saw she wasn't, he took the paper he had from under his arm. 'Let me see now,' he said, shaking it out to look at the front page. 'It is Saturday, the seventh of September. 1940,' he added, with a little sideways grin.

1940. That was during the war, the Second World War. Wasn't it?

'Thank you.' Rose wanted to say more, but she couldn't, she didn't know what to say. So she just stood there, watching the tall, slim figure move off towards the station, people turning to stare at him as he passed. And then:

'Wuff!'

Tommy was wagging his tail and sneezing with excitement. He'd spotted someone coming out of the station, someone holding the hand of a little girl with fair plaits. Rose felt her stomach clench. Because it was her. The girl in the photograph with the dark curls and the red lipstick and the mischievous expression.

It was Rosemary. The girl who would grow up to be Rose's Aunt Cosy. And she was heading straight for Johnny.

Rose held her breath. *Was this why her aunt had brought her here, back to the London of her youth? So she could see the moment that she and Johnny met?*

Closer they got, closer. Any minute now they would see each other and the world would change for both of them.

And then the little girl dropped the toy monkey she was clutching and Johnny stopped to let an old lady go past and the moment was gone. Rosemary bent down to pick up the monkey, Johnny hurried off into the station and it was over. They hadn't met after all.

Rose felt suddenly desperate. Was it her fault? Maybe if she hadn't been there, if she hadn't stepped into the road at just that moment, if Johnny hadn't stopped to save her, he and Rosemary would have met. Had she ruined everything for them? Had she somehow managed to change the course of history?

'Sorry, 'scuse us.'

Rosemary was pushing past, heading away from the station. She looked young, about the same age as Rose, and seemed tired and preoccupied, but the little girl turned and stared at Tommy with big eyes as he wagged his tail. They headed away past the shop with the single sad dish of sweets in the window and around the corner. They were going home, Rose realised. Home to Nightingale Lane.

So she followed them.

The crowds thinned out as they turned the corner and hurried away from the shops and into the long stretch of Nightingale Lane. It seemed much wider than Rose remembered (probably because there were no parked cars) and the houses had a tired look as if they were waiting for a fresh coat of paint. The old school hadn't changed though, and the pub even had the same sign: a picture of a chubby brown bird (a nightingale, Rose presumed, because that was the pub's name) sitting in a tree. As they walked past, an old man in a flat cap came out and spat on the pavement.

Although the little girl turned to stare at them a couple more times, Rosemary (Rose couldn't think of this girl as her aunt!) didn't seem to notice they were there. Until they got to the house, when she stopped and wheeled round so quickly that Rose almost bumped into her.

'Are you following us?' Her dark eyes were glittering with amusement.

Rose didn't know what to say. This girl – *Rosemary* – can't have been much older than her, but she seemed so much more confident. So much more grown-up.

She looked down at the little girl who smiled a secret smile and hid her face in Rosemary's coat. Her monkey waved a paw at Rose, who realised it was a glove puppet and waved a finger back.

'My monkey likes your dog,' the little girl said, emerging from the coat. 'He's called Munk-munk. What's your dog's name?'

Tommy wagged his tail and grinned, but before Rose could reply, he stopped. His ears went up and he stood quite still, listening with his whole body, just like he had done on the common with Aunt Cosy.

'Tom?' Rose said. 'What's up? What can you—'

She was interrupted by a mournful wail that curled up into the air, getting louder and closer, louder and closer, rising and falling as if it contained all the sadness in the world. Rose felt cold in spite of the warmth of the afternoon. It wasn't, was it? Not when the sun was shining and the sky was so very blue. *It couldn't be the air raid warning.*

But it was. Rose could tell by the look on Rosemary's face. She was frowning and biting her lip as the last note sank away into the air.

'Cosy?' The little girl was tugging at her hand. 'Munk-munk doesn't like the siren. He thinks it sounds sad.'

'Well, you tell him not to worry,' said Rosemary. She was rummaging in her bag. 'It'll just be another false alarm. But still, we'd better go in.'

She found her keys and turned to the door. The little girl looked longingly at Tommy and held out the monkey as if she wanted to give it to him. Rosemary tugged at her hand.

'Come on, Betty. Let's—'

And then she stopped. All of them stopped dead, as if they'd been turned to stone. Because they all heard it.

Where are you? Where are you? Where are you?

The rhythm of engines, coming closer and closer, making the ground beneath their feet vibrate. Rose looked up at the sky, afraid of what she was going to see.

And there they were.

The sky was full of planes. Row after row after row of them, silvery and glittering in the sunlight, sliding past like a great shoal of fish, the big planes hemmed in by smaller ones. Rose could see black crosses on the underside of their wings. There must have been three hundred of the big planes, more of the little ones. They just kept on coming, in strict formation, forwards, forwards, forwards. They just kept on coming.

Where are you?

Rosemary was staring too and the little girl was holding up her monkey to watch as the planes slid past. An elderly woman wearing slippers and a flowery apron had appeared on the doorstep of the house next door and a man with a rolled umbrella had paused on the pavement opposite and was looking up with a hurt and puzzled expression. It seemed as if the whole of the city was watching the sky.

'So they're coming.' The old woman shook her head at the planes as if she was disappointed in them. 'They said they would. And now they are. Blighters.'

Rose wasn't sure whether the blighters were the planes or the people who'd said they'd come.

'Where are our fighters?' the woman went on. 'That's what I want to know. Where's the blinking RAF?'

'Someone's going to cop it tonight.' A young man on a bicycle with some sort of tatty black instrument case strapped to the back had stopped in the middle of the road. He had a skinny neck and spots on his chin and he sounded almost pleased.

'Shut your face, Billy Boyce,' said Rosemary. 'Could be your house gets it.'

He blushed from the neck upwards. 'I was only saying—'

'Well, don't!' She fixed him with an angry glare. 'Don't say! We don't want to hear it! Do we, Mrs Wetherington?'

Mrs Wetherington shook her head. 'First war finished, we thought that was it. And now look.' She gestured up at the planes with disgust. 'I'm too old for this,' she said, and went back into her house, shutting the door behind her.

And still the planes kept coming.

'Where are they going, Cosy?' said the little girl. She was making her monkey wave a paw to the planes as they went past.

'I don't know, Bets. The docks, I expect. Doesn't look like they're interested in us. But we best not take the risk.' She looked at Rose. 'You better come too.'

'Really?' said Rose. 'Are you sure?'

Rosemary shrugged. 'Well, we can't leave you out here, can we?' she said. 'And, correct me if I'm wrong, but I get the feeling you've got nowhere else to—'

BAM! BAM-BAM! BAM!

The noise was like nothing Rose had ever heard. It seemed to come from all around them, as if the whole of London was shouting with rage at the sky, bellowing and barking like a huge angry dog chained up in a backyard. The little girl laughed with delight and started to tap-dance on the pavement along with the rhythm of the bangs while the young man jumped on his bike and sped off down the road.

'What's going on?' Rose had to shout to be heard.

Rosemary stared at her. 'It's our big guns of course, the ones on the common. You must have heard them before?' She looked up at the sky. 'That's it!' she shouted. 'Give 'em socks!'

The blue of the sky was criss-crossed with streams of black smoke shooting up towards the planes.

'Come on!' Rosemary grabbed her sister's arm and dragged her into the house, leaving the door open for Rose and Tommy. 'It's this way!'

They ran through the hallway, past the cuckoo clock in its place on the wall, through the kitchen with an unfamiliar old cooker and clutter of silvery saucepans, and out down the garden path to the Anderson shelter.

Rose and Tommy didn't need to be told where to go. After all, this was their house too.

6

Rose and Tommy followed the little girl as she tumbled down the concrete steps into the shelter. It felt chilly after the warmth of the sunshine outside and it took a moment for Rose's eyes to adjust to the grainy darkness.

The shelter was much nicer than when she'd last seen it. There was a bunk bed, each bunk covered in colourful knitted blankets, and a wooden crate at the end that was being used as a table, with a pile of books and magazines and a framed photograph of a young man in uniform. There was even a small camping stove, with a kettle and tea things on a tin tray next to it on the floor.

Rosemary closed the door behind them, shutting out the sunshine. The noise of the guns was muffled and seemed less real now. Less frightening. It didn't seem to bother Rosemary or her sister at all now they were in the shelter, even though Rose's heart was thudding so loud she was afraid they might be able to hear it.

'Where's Mummy?' The little girl had scrambled up

on to the top bunk and was swinging her legs.

'She's doing a late shift at the factory, Betty, you know that. She'll have gone to the shelter there. Come here, dog.' Rosemary held out her hand to Tommy, who trotted over and sniffed it.

'What's your name?' she said, scratching him in his favourite place behind the ears.

'It's Tommy,' said Rose.

Rosemary let out a little shout of laughter that sounded so exactly like Aunt Cosy that Rose felt her skin prickle. 'Not *his* name!' she said. 'Yours!'

Rose felt her cheeks burn. 'Rose,' she said, hoping that there'd be no more questions. How could she explain who she was or how she got there? She didn't know herself.

'Rose?!' Betty hung her head upside down over the edge of the bunk so her plaits dangled. 'That's funny, isn't it, Cosy? She looks like you and she's got nearly the same name!'

'Does she look like me?' Rosemary squinted at Rose in the gloom. 'Ah well, it happens, I suppose. All sorts of people look like other people.'

'Mrs Wetherington looks like Mr Churchill,' said Betty.

'You're right,' said Rosemary. 'I'd love to see him in one of her hats, wouldn't you? "We shall fight on the beaches",' she said, doing a funny voice. '"We shall never surrender!"'

'And Billy Boyce looks like a chicken.' Betty clambered down from the top bunk and squatted next to Tommy.

'Don't be horrid, Betty,' said Rosemary. But she giggled and this time Rose couldn't help joining in. The young man with the bike did look a bit like a chicken,

43

with his skinny neck and anxious beady eyes. 'I'm Rosemary, by the way. And this creature is my sister Betty.' Rose shook the hand she held out and looked into those familiar eyes.

Is this really happening? she thought. *Am I really in an Anderson shelter with Aunt Cosy as a young girl? During the Second World War?* The thought made her feel queasy and faint, as if she'd been twirling on the little roundabout in the playground for too long or playing twizzles with Grace and Ella after school.

Betty leant over to confide in a loud whisper. 'Billy Boyce loves Cosy!'

'He does not! Betty! If you say that one more time, I swear I will strangle that monkey!'

'Do you have someone though?' The words tumbled out before Rose could stop them. She wouldn't usually be brave enough to come out with a question like that, especially with someone she didn't know. But then she *did* know Rosemary, of course she did. She'd known her all her life. Rosemary stopped trying to grab her sister's monkey and Betty took the opportunity to escape with him to the top bunk.

'A young man, you mean?'

Rose nodded.

'Nope.' Rosemary sounded very definite. 'You?'

Rose thought of Fred and the message she'd sent him before all this had started. 'No,' she said. 'I just thought that maybe . . .' She looked at the photograph propped up on the crate.

'Him?' Rosemary laughed again. 'That's our dad!'

'Oh, what? Sorry. I didn't know . . .'

'No reason why you should. Our father was one of the men who didn't die in the last war.' Rosemary looked at the photo. 'I'm just glad he's not around to see this one.'

'Is he—?'

Rosemary nodded. 'Soon after Bets was born. His lungs had never been good. He was gassed, you know, in the trenches.' She tapped the back of Rose's hand, just like Aunt Cosy did when she wanted her full attention. 'Do you know what Mother said when they made the announcement on the wireless last year? You know, "This country is at war with Germany" and all that?' Rose shook her head. 'She was standing at the sink washing up the breakfast things and she dropped the dishcloth and looked at the ceiling and said, "Not again." Not again!'

Rosemary drew back to watch Rose's reaction. Rose didn't know what to say. Rosemary seemed somehow more alive than anyone she'd ever met. Maybe it was the war made her like that. If you didn't know what was going to happen tomorrow, maybe you had to make the most of today.

'Which is why,' Rosemary was saying, 'I most definitely do not want a young man. Oh I do, in a way, you know – but not now. Not when he could go off somewhere and never come back. I don't think I could bear that. Could you?'

Before Rose could reply, Betty hung her head down from the top bunk again. 'Can I have your dog?' she said. 'We used to have one, called Sophie, but she died.'

Sophie, thought Rose. *That was what Aunt Cosy always called Tom.* She wondered where Aunt Cosy was now. Was she really out there somewhere, lost in the wartime London of her memory? Or had Rose just imagined she'd seen her standing there under the big plane tree on the corner of the common?

'Don't be daft, Bets,' said Rosemary. 'He's Rose's dog.'

Betty squatted on the floor and made her monkey stroke Tommy's back with one paw. 'Are there any biscuits?' she said.

Rosemary felt about beneath the bunk and brought out a tin box, pale blue with a pattern of pink roses. There was no rust and the colours were fresh and new, but there was no mistaking it. It was Aunt Cosy's memory box.

'A few,' said Rosemary, looking inside. 'Not very nice.' She offered the tin to Betty, who took two and gave one to Tommy. 'Rose?'

As she held out the tin, a terrible tearing whistling sound cut through the air. It sounded as if the sky was being torn in half like an old sheet. And then—

THUNK.

A deep, echoing thud that Rose felt in the pit of her stomach. The whole world seemed to shift and shudder. Then, silence.

Nobody said anything, not even Betty. They sat quite still and looked at each other's faces as dust floated down from the roof of the shelter like snow. And then, quietly at first, Rosemary started to sing:

'*I know where I'm going . . .*'

Rose felt her skin prickle. It was the voice that she'd heard every evening since she'd moved into the house on Nightingale Lane.

'*And I know who's going with me . . .*'

Betty got up and sat on the bunk very close to her sister, watching Rosemary's face as she sang. Her voice grew louder and more confident as it frightened their fears away.

'*I know who I love, but I don't know who I'll marry . . .*'

'Except we *do* know who Cosy's going to marry, don't we? She's going to marry Billy Boyce!'

'I am not!' Rosemary stopped singing and tried to grab

Betty's monkey. 'You are a horrid little girl!'

As she watched the two girls tussling together, Rose felt a pang. This was what it was like to have a sister. All she was going to get was a stupid stepbrother she didn't even like.

'We're not afraid of the silly old bombs, are we, Munk-munk?' said Betty as Rosemary gave up and collapsed laughing on the bunk. Her monkey shook his head and started to sing in Betty's voice:

'*It's a long way to TippeRAReee . . .*'

'I know you're not afraid, Betty, you're as brave as a lion, that's the whole trouble. Sit down and eat your biscuit. We've got to wait for the all-clear. Come on, Rose, you have one too. We don't know how long it'll be.'

Rose took a biscuit. Rosemary was right – it was hard and not very nice. She looked up as she crunched, feeling Rosemary's eyes on her.

'Are you a local girl, Rose?' she said. 'I've not seen you around here before.'

Rose swallowed a large chunk of biscuit. 'Yes,' she said. The biscuit seemed to have got stuck halfway down. 'I am in a way. Local, I mean.' She took a deep breath. 'I'm looking for someone actually. That's what I was doing when I saw you coming out of the tube station.' Rose pictured Aunt Cosy, wandering round in the tangle of her memories while she sat there, eating biscuits in the shelter. 'Listen, I should go. I've got to find her.'

'You can't go anywhere until the all-clear. Have another biscuit.'

'There's none left,' said Betty. She was sitting on the floor, cuddling Tommy. Munk-munk was balanced on his back like a jockey riding a horse. 'I've been giving them

47

to Tommy.'

'Betty . . .' Rosemary shook her head at her, but Betty was looking at Rose.

'I love him,' she said. Her eyes were green with very dark eyelashes in spite of her fair hair. 'He's a special dog, isn't he?'

'Yes,' said Rose. 'He is. Very special.'

The Very Special Dog grinned and wagged his tail as he felt the three pairs of eyes on him, looking pleased but embarrassed to be the object of so much attention. Then, something changed. Munk-munk slid to the ground as Tommy stood up, ears pricked, listening.

'What's he doing?' said Betty.

'Shh.' Rose couldn't hear anything, but she knew she would. 'Dogs always hear things first.' She knew that now.

And then it came. A long, constant blast of sound filled up the air, as if someone somewhere was leaning on a giant car horn.

'That's the all-clear!' Rosemary scrambled to her feet. 'Come on, girls, let's inspect the damage.'

Betty beat her to the door. She scrambled up the steps and pushed it open, letting a dusty sunbeam into the shelter. Tommy skittered after her as she danced across the lawn, monkey on her hand and plaits flying. Rose was somehow surprised to emerge into a world that didn't look very different. Dark-green shadows stretched across the grass and the air glittered with dust.

'What's that smell?' said Rose. It was like when a match is blown out.

'I don't know.' Rosemary flung back her head to look at the sky. It was blue and perfectly clear. 'Smoke?' she said. 'Is that what bombs smell like? We've not had one so close before.' She looked at the house. 'No damage done that I can see. The blast can't have been near enough to break the windows.'

Betty grabbed her hand and pulled her towards the door that led through to the street. 'I want to see what's happened!'

There were some bits of twisted metal lying on the road that Tommy sniffed at, but otherwise it looked the same as before. Other people were emerging from their front doors, looking dazed, as if they too were surprised to find that the world was still there and the sun still shining.

'Not as bad as it sounded then.' Mrs Wetherington was at her front door. 'They didn't get us this time. Blighters. I tell you, if I could get my hands on that ruddy Adolf . . .'

Rose suppressed a giggle as Rosemary caught her eye. Betty was right, Mrs Wetherington did look like Winston Churchill.

'Shrapnel!' Betty had picked up one of the bits of twisted metal and was banging it against the wall.

'Put that down, Betty! It might be sharp!'

Betty threw it into the road just as the young man with the bike skidded to a halt beside them. He was wearing overalls now, navy blue, and a tin helmet with a big letter W on it. His face was grey with dust.

'All right, Billy?' said Rosemary. 'Where was the bomb?'

'Couple of streets away,' he said. 'Family bombed out, but nobody hurt this time. I've taken them to the rescue centre. We got it easy. Unlike some.'

He pointed to the horizon. The sky above them was clear, but away over the rooftops across the road there was a great cloud that rolled and shifted as if it was alive, glowing red and orange and pink.

Rosemary reached for Betty's hand. 'That's the sun

going down.' She gave the young man a quick, frightened look. 'Isn't it?'

'In the east?' he said. 'That's no sunset, Rosemary. That's the East End. It's on fire.'

7

'I've got to go,' said Rose.

'What?' said Rosemary. She sounded almost cross. 'Where? Why? *Why* have you got to go?'

Rose thought of Aunt Cosy standing under the plane tree on the corner of Clapham Common. She didn't know if the old lady was still out there somewhere, wandering the streets of the burning city in her dressing gown and slippers, but she did know one thing: she couldn't just stay here, doing nothing. She had to find out.

'Hey!' Rosemary was moving her hand in front of Rose's face. Her lipstick had worn off, which made her look younger and even more like Rose. 'Have you even got somewhere to go to?'

Rose shook her head, trying to choke back the teary feeling she was getting behind her eyes. 'Not really,' she said.

'I knew it! I knew there was something lost about you.'

'What d'you mean?'

'You've been bombed out, haven't you?' Rosemary turned to the young man with the bike. 'Billy – this is one for you.'

It was the first time Billy had looked at Rose properly. 'Is that right?' His voice was gentler than before. 'Have you – lost someone? Can I ask?'

Rose knew what he meant but chose to misunderstand him. 'Yes,' she said. 'I have. An old lady. My aunt.' It was true, of course, just not in the way that Billy meant.

'I'm sorry,' said Billy. He sounded like he really was and Rose felt bad. 'Got any other people?' he went on. 'Mother? Dad?'

Dad. He suddenly appeared in Rose's memory, as clear as day, standing at their front door, waving goodbye as she ran down the road to meet her friends on the corner to go to school. He was wearing an apron, the one with blue and white stripes, and still had the washing-up brush in his hand. Grandad always used to tell Rose never to wave someone out of sight. If you did, he said – if you carried on waving until you couldn't see them any more – you'd wave them out of your life. And he was right. Dad did wave himself out of Rose's life that day. She never saw him again. She'd looked back and wiggled her fingers at him in a little 'OK, Dad, you can go in now' wave, before hitching her bag on to her shoulder and heading off with Grace and Ella. She hadn't looked back again. But she'd always wished she had.

Rose blinked and looked at Billy Boyce's face, grey with dust under his helmet. The spots on his chin made him look young, probably younger than he was. He reminded her of the boys in her year at school, the ones who were good with computers and bad at talking to girls.

'No, nobody else,' she said. 'Not – not here anyway.

Just my aunt.'

'We could check the homeless persons' register if you like. The – hospitals?' He looked down at the pavement. 'Where did you last see her? Was she in the house when it happened? When the bomb—'

'No,' said Rose. 'It wasn't like that.' How could she tell him that she suspected her aunt was out there somewhere, lost in the web of her own memories, and that she, Rose, had not the least idea of how to find her? He'd just think she was mad. 'It's OK. I'll find her myself.'

She turned to go, but Billy grabbed her arm.

'You should be in a shelter tonight,' he said. 'They'll be back as soon as it gets dark.'

Rosemary was watching Betty who was drawing a picture of a dog on the pavement with a bit of chalky stone. She looked up sharply. 'What makes you say that, Bill?'

'RAF can't see in the dark, can they?'

'Of course.' She looked over the rooftops at the angry glow in the sky. 'And the whole of the East End is lit up like a blinking Christmas tree.'

The three of them stood in silence for a second.

'Yup,' said Billy. 'The Luftwaffe won't have any trouble finding that in the dark. So they'll come back and give them some more.'

'Poor people.' Rosemary bit her lip. Her face looked very pale in the evening light. 'I wish there was something I could do.'

'Like what?'

'I don't know. Warden, like you, Billy. Fire service, ambulance driver. Something.'

'Can you drive?'

'No, but—' She frowned. Then, 'Nurse! I could be a nurse.'

Billy laughed, which made her furious.

'I could!' she said. 'I'd be a blooming good nurse, Billy Boyce! Why wouldn't I?'

'I don't know, Rosemary, I can't see it. No, tell you what, you want to help people, you stick to what you're good at. You've got a nice voice on you, use your talent. Sing to them.'

'Are you trying to be funny?' She narrowed her eyes. 'Is this another way of getting me to sing with that band of yours?'

'No! People are doing it, musicians and stuff. Singers. They go down the shelters. Bucks everyone up no end. We had a woman playing a cello the other night.'

Betty looked up from her drawing. 'What's a cello?'

'A very big violin,' said her sister. But Rose could see that Billy's suggestion had got her interested. 'What do they do, then? Just turn up and start?'

'Yup. One bloke read poems. That didn't go down so well, the kids threw buns. Usually, though, people are ever so grateful.'

'I could sing to them!' Betty shouted. '*It's a long way to Tipper-RAR-ree! It's a long way to go—*'

'Stop it, Bets, nobody's going to do any singing tonight.' Rosemary looked at the sky again and turned to Rose, who was standing a little apart from them on the pavement. 'What do you want to do, Rose?'

Rose took a deep breath. 'I'll go with Billy,' she said. 'I really do need to find my aunt.'

'But we'll see you again?'

'Not if we see her first!' shouted Betty.

'Shut up, Bets. Rose?' Rosemary held out her hand.

Rose took it and looked into the familiar eyes of the girl who was to become her Aunt Cosy. The face around them wasn't the same, this one was young and fresh and

54

lovely. But the eyes hadn't changed at all. They were still dark, shiny brown, like those of a mouse.

'Good luck,' said Rosemary.

Rose nodded. Across the road a woman walked past pushing a big black pram.

Billy was in a hurry to go now. 'Come on,' he said. 'I'm on duty tonight, and we need to get you to a shelter before the blackout.' He looked down at Tommy. 'That your dog? Not allowed in the shelter, I'm afraid. He'll have to stay here.'

Rose's heart lurched. She didn't think she could bear it, being alone in this city without Tommy. But she had to. She knew they'd find each other again. It was like Betty said, Tommy was a special dog.

'Betty?' She squatted down on the pavement next to the little girl. 'Will you look after Tommy for me, please? Just till I get back?'

'When will that be?' said Betty. 'Perhaps NEVER?!'

Rose looked up at Rosemary. 'Will that be all right with your mum?'

Rosemary nodded. 'But he's your dog. Are you sure?'

'I'm sure.' He'd probably be safer with them than out on the streets in the dark. Rose put her arm round him and hid her face in his rough fur. 'And you, Mr Thomas,' she said, her voice sounding false and squeaky as she tried not to cry, 'you look after Betty. Will you?' He wagged his tail once, twice, three times and stuck his wet nose in her ear. 'I'll see you soon.'

And then she got up and followed Billy Boyce as he pushed his bike up Nightingale Lane towards Clapham Common. Behind them, Rosemary and her sister started singing: '*It's a long way to Tipper-RAR-ry! It's a long way to go . . .*'

And, just like when she'd said goodbye to her dad for

the last time, Rose didn't look back.

'I'll have to leave you here,' said Billy when they reached the end of Nightingale Lane. 'You know how to get to the shelter?'

Rose nodded. She didn't, of course, but she wasn't going to tell him that. She watched him as he rode off down the street, leaving her standing there on her own, wondering what to do.

The sight of the common spread out in the late evening sunshine reminded her of the thousand and one times she'd gone there with her friends after school, swinging along its paths with school bags over their shoulders, or lying on the grass staring at the sky. If it wasn't for the unfamiliar smell of burnt matches in the air and those strange silvery balloons floating above the trees, she could almost imagine she was on her way to meet Grace and Ella in the cafe, to share a single mug of hot chocolate and a hundred funny stories about school and parents and boys . . .

That was before Dad died, of course, before Mum announced that she was getting married. It was usually just Rose and Tommy who walked on the common now.

And Aunt Cosy.

And just as that thought dropped into Rose's mind, she saw her. Standing under the big plane tree across the road, in her blue dressing gown and red velvet slippers, looking straight at her.

Aunt Cosy.

Rose kept her eyes on her, willing her to stay where she was, afraid that if she lost sight of her for one second she would disappear again. A black cab rumbled past, familiar, with its yellow light feeble in the sunshine.

'Aunt Cosy!'

The little figure had turned and was beetling away into the glimmering dusk.

'Wait!'

Her aunt was heading along the path that led into the heart of the huge stretch of open parkland that was the common. Rose ran across the road and set off after her, past one of the huge silvery balloons, anchored by its heavy steel cable to a concrete base, past an area where it looked like people were growing vegetables, towards the centre of the common. She could see the outlines of the big guns in the distance, the ones they'd heard earlier, she assumed. They were silent now, but ready, pointing at the sky.

Rose stopped for a moment to catch her breath, her heart beating all over her body. The evening sunlight glittered with drifting particles of dust and thistledown and when she looked up, the little figure was disappearing into a group of trees. She ran after her, around a bend in the path, through the trees and there it was, the bandstand, with Aunt Cosy sitting on its steps.

Rose stopped. Then, as she took her first step towards her—

BAM. BAM. BAM.

The world flashed white-hot with terror.

BAM-BAM.

The sound vibrated deep inside her body. She looked up and saw trails of black smoke streaked across the deep blue of the sky like angry scribbles. Beyond them, a group of German planes floated soundlessly, too high for Rose to hear their engines.

BAM.

There was that smell of burnt matches again, and something else, something that reminded Rose of evenings with Mum in the days before Sal when they'd sit in front of the telly together and Mum would brush Rose's hair. Sometimes they'd do proper makeovers, with face packs and nail varnish and – *nail varnish remover*. That was it, that strange chokey smell that caught in your throat and left a sweet, chemical taste in your mouth. That was what she could smell now.

BAM-BAM-BAM.

Another blast. Another spurt of black smoke. Another useless explosion that left the planes drifting peacefully on their way, too high for the guns to reach. Maybe they were heading home to Germany. Rose hoped so. She thought of the men inside, going back to their mums and wives and girlfriends, and she was glad.

And then it was over. The planes had gone and the guns were quiet. Rose took a long, shuddering breath and turned back to the bandstand.

Aunt Cosy had disappeared.

Rose looked around, left, right, everywhere, but there was no one around. No little figure disappearing over the horizon or into the trees. Although the guns had sounded very close, the common seemed deserted. The birds were singing again, the blue of the evening was thickening into dusk and Rose felt terribly alone. *I don't belong here,* she thought, *in this wartime London.* But she didn't really belong in the other one either, the one where her dad didn't exist any more and her mum was getting married to another man.

She stumbled over to the bandstand, flopped down on the steps where she'd last seen Aunt Cosy, and felt in her pocket for her phone. The battery was low and there was no signal here, of course, but it was still working. She looked at the last message she'd sent, the one where she'd told Fred not to come to the wedding. Maybe he hadn't read it yet. Maybe she should never have sent it.

It was too late now.

She wished he was there, so she could explain. Tell him how she was feeling bad about the wedding, embarrassed that her grandad had asked him to travel so far, worried he wouldn't want to come or would think she was pushy and needy and sad. And he would smile his slow smile and shake his head and say, 'I didn't see the message anyway. My phone was turned off, I was at the movies with my friends,' and Rose would feel silly for having made a fuss, but happy that things were still all right between them.

Fred always made everything seem all right, even when it wasn't, *especially* when it wasn't. But he wasn't here. He was at home in Berlin in the twenty-first century, miles and miles and years and years away and he hadn't replied to her message. Even a photo of him would have made her feel better, smiling his serious smile and squinting at the camera, his fair hair flopping over his gentle blue eyes. But she'd never had the chance to take one because they hadn't seen each other again, not since the time they'd first met in Belgium. They'd talked on Skype a couple of times, but had both found it too weird, so had agreed to stick to messaging.

She'd never have a photo of him now.

She scrolled through the other pictures on her phone. There were loads of pictures of Tommy, head on one side, looking interested, enthusiastic and a bit puzzled, like he always did; some old ones of Grace and Ella making kissy faces at the camera; one of Rose herself, trying to be mysterious and just looking like she needed to go to the loo; Mum in the kitchen in her dressing gown, hiding her face with her hand because it was first thing in the morning and she thought she looked old; Aunt Cosy, sitting in her special chair, turning to the camera because

Rose had just called her name.

Aunt Cosy? Aunty Coseeee!

Rose smiled at the photo, remembering the day she took it. It seemed a very long time ago that she'd followed her aunt out of the house and down into the underground at Clapham South. The sun felt warm on her face and she lay back on the step with her head in the hood of her parka and closed her eyes.

Somewhere, in the quiet of the evening, the fox barked.

8

Rose was woken by something wet spattering on her face. She opened her eyes and at first could see nothing, nothing at all. And then, as she stared into the solid darkness, she saw one tiny point of light, a pinprick in a black velvet curtain. As she gazed, afraid to take her eyes off it in case it disappeared, it winked at her. And then she saw another and another and another and she realised that she was looking at the night sky.

And it was raining.

Rose lay there for a moment, feeling the rain on her face and gazing up into the star-studded darkness. She'd never seen the sky like that before, not in London. That was because of light pollution, Grandad had told her. The city was so brightly lit that all you could see was the orange glow of the street lights reflected on the sky. You couldn't see the stars. Rose shivered. It had been warm when she'd fallen asleep in the sun on that September evening in 1940, but it was cold now, really cold.

Is it still autumn? Rose wondered. *Is it still 1940?*

Is the war still going on?

And then, just as she was hoping it might all be over:
NoooooooOOOOOOOoooooooOOOOOOooooo . . .

She recognised it now, the way it began with a sad intake of breath and then spread out, up and down, up and down, in its desperate drawn-out wail. The air raid warning.

As if in response to the sound, three great beams of white light sliced up through the sky, moving and criss-crossing each other, stroking the darkness like giant fingers. And then another sound joined the siren's wail:
Where are you? Where are you? Where are you?

One of the lights picked up the outline of a single plane, high up above the rain. The other beams honed in on it and held it like an insect pinned against the sky.
Where are you? Where are—
BAM! BAM-BAM!

The guns started up, shouting their fury at the tiny plane. Rose was on her feet now, searching her pockets for her phone, to put on the torch, give herself some light. But there was no need. Silvery lights started dropping from the sky, sparkling like fireworks, falling with a strange popping sound and spreading their ghostly white light over the common. Rose started to run, back the way she'd come when she'd followed Aunt Cosy, back towards the road, back to where there might be a shelter.

Just in time.

Because there was another sound, a sound that seemed to tear straight through her body. It was the same terrible whistling scream that she'd heard in the shelter with Rosemary and Betty, but this time it was much louder, much closer, much much more terrifying. Rose didn't stop to think, there was no time. She threw herself on to the ground, her face on the path, gravel in her mouth, digging into her cheek. And waited for the blast.

It didn't come. The ground shook, jerking and juddering beneath her as if it was alive, but there was no explosion. The seconds slid past and Rose waited, with the night roaring all around her, until the guns had stopped their furious barking. She got up, gravel from the path sticking to her face, and started to run again.

She wasn't sure how far she'd gone, she just knew she couldn't go any further. She doubled up, trying to catch her breath, afraid she might be sick, barely conscious of the white-painted edge of the pavement opposite and the dim light that came from the entrance to the station. A few people hurried through the darkness like shadows, shining their torches down at the pavement so they could see where they were going.

And it was still raining.

Once Rose's breathing had slowed down, she found the torch on her phone and crossed the road, making for the station entrance. Didn't people use the stations to shelter from air raids in the war? She was sure she'd heard that somewhere. It would certainly feel safer down there, deep beneath the ground. There might even be a train, she thought. A train that could take her home, back to the twenty-first century.

'You can't go in there, sweetheart.' A man stopped her at the station entrance. He was wearing the same sort of boiler suit and tin helmet as Billy.

'What?' Rose looked up at him. His face was tired and grey and he needed a shave.

'No trains running. Not now. They've closed this station for the night.'

'But—'

'You'll have to go to Balham. They're letting people shelter there.'

63

'*Balham?*'

'You'll get there in a few minutes if you hurry. Follow the road round and—'

'I know the way!' Rose felt bad as soon as the words came out. She hadn't meant to snap. 'Sorry,' she said, then stopped. 'This is going to sound really stupid, but I'm a bit confused. Can you tell me what the date is?'

'The date?' The man stared at her. 'It's the fourteenth of October, love. Monday. The start of a brand-new week.'

'1940?'

He looked at her to see if she was joking. 'Yup, it's still 1940, worse luck. Roll on '41, I say.'

'Thanks,' said Rose. 'Sorry. I'm just . . . sorry.'

But as she turned to walk away—

CLACK! CLACK-CLACK!

Things were dropping from the sky again, lighting up the rain-streaked darkness and turning the street into a black-and-white photo of itself. One landed with a sharp crack on the road right beside Rose. As she stared, it started to fizz and crackle with a lurid white light, jerking about on the ground as if it was alive.

'Stand back, love,' said the man. 'This one's got my name on.'

He took his helmet off and approached it cautiously, putting one foot carefully in front of the other as if he was afraid it would bite him, and then, in one sudden movement, threw his helmet over it as if it was a spider he was catching beneath a glass.

'Gotcha!' he said and grinned at Rose as he stood there, holding the helmet in place with one foot. 'That's one that won't hurt anybody tonight.'

'One what?' said Rose. 'What is that thing?'

The man stared at her. 'Incendiary bomb,' he said.

'They're all right if you get to them in time. Bucket of sand's best.' He grinned. 'Or you can always jump on 'em if you've got a good enough pair of boots.' He kicked the helmet away, then, using the edge of his sleeve to protect his hand from the heat, picked it up and made his way back to the station entrance.

'What happens if you don't get to them in time?'

The man shrugged and got out a packet of cigarettes. 'London burns down,' he said and lit a match.

Rose hurried off down the High Road, finding her way as best she could by the feeble light from her phone. The battery wasn't going to last much longer. As she got nearer Balham station, the pavements filled up with shadowy figures, all hurrying in the same direction. There were some older people, their shoulders hunched against the rain, and women with children who looked dazed with sleep, mothers laden down with blankets and bundles and babies. Some of the younger children were clutching cuddly toys, stuffed rabbits and teddy bears, worn out with kisses. Big sisters held the hands of little ones, older boys carried bags and tried not to look scared. The old men were grey-faced, tight-lipped, silent, trudging through the darkness. They'd seen this all before.

And still the planes came over and the guns barked at the sky.

Rose felt a surge of relief as the station appeared, its low shape looming up out of the gloom. It looked familiar, in its place at the crossroads, in spite of the sandbags piled up against the walls. She hurried across the road to the entrance, slipping through the crowd, and made her way into the ticket hall. A kind-faced woman in a tin helmet waved her through the barrier and Rose joined the others, standing in silence on the creaky wooden escalator.

Down they went, into the gloomy depths below the street. There was an earthy smell of damp clothes and not very clean people and a whiff of public toilets that caught you in the back of the throat and got stronger the further down you went. There were people everywhere at the bottom, sitting propped up against the tiled walls or lying down, covered in blankets and rugs, their heads on rolled-up coats or small suitcases. Mothers whispered to their children, stroking their heads, others had brought flasks of tea and sandwiches as if they were on some strange underground picnic. An old man sat on a camping stool and stared straight ahead, holding a tin mug of tea against his chest with both hands. A woman glanced up as Rose stepped over a sleeping child and then went back to turning the pages of her magazine. And then:

'*I know where I'm going . . .*'

It was the voice Rose had heard every evening since they'd moved into the house on Nightingale Lane. The voice she'd heard in the Anderson shelter on that sunny afternoon when the planes flew over London and the bombs rained down on the East End.

'*And I know who's going with me . . .*'

She followed the sound through to one of the platforms, the northbound one. It was even more crowded there and you had to be careful where you put your feet to avoid standing on somebody. An old man was already snoring, propped up against the wall, his legs covered in a grubby-looking bedspread printed with smudgy pink roses. Everything looked faded and old and shabby, blankets were grey and pinkish and beige; faces, white and expressionless, turned in the same direction as they listened to the song.

'*I know who I love . . .*'

It was Rosemary. She was standing at the end of the

platform, wearing dark-blue or black trousers and jacket, with her curls held back by some sort of hairband or scarf. Her lipstick was very red, her face very pale. She seemed somehow more real than the faded people on the platform, more solid, as if they were an audience in a dream.

'*But I don't know who I'll marry . . .*'

Rose turned suddenly. It was as if somebody had called her name or tapped her on the shoulder, although she knew they hadn't. And there, at the far end of the platform, shimmering in the gloom, was Aunt Cosy in her silky dressing gown and red velvet slippers, smiling as she watched her younger self singing to the people.

'*Some say he's bad but I say he's bonny . . .*'

A few of the other women joined in with the last words of the song.

'*The fairest of them all, my handsome, winsome Johnny.*'

There was a little pause like a sigh as the people let the final notes sink away into the gloom. Then, another voice, a squeaky out-of-tune one, shattered the moment.

'*It's a long way to TippeRARy, it's a long way to go—*'

Betty. Everyone burst out laughing, including Rosemary. Rose saw mothers hugging their children, old men grinning, showing mouthfuls of bad teeth, old women rolling their eyes and shaking their heads.

She didn't hear the explosion.

The lights went out. The darkness was complete. And the screams started.

Rose found herself on the ground, her face pressed up against something hard that she realised was a shoe. She couldn't tell if there was a foot inside it. She tried to get up, but there were people moving around her in the darkness, pushing, falling, trampling. She was knocked down again. Somebody trod on her hand. There were shouts in the dark.

'Where are you?'

'Mother!'

'Where are you?'

'Over here!'

'Mummy!'

And then there was a great WHOOOMPH and a crash and a rushing sound. And—

Water.

Water?

In the middle of the screams and the chaos and the terror, Rose's mind went: *How can there be water? We're nowhere near the river.* But there was. She couldn't see it, but you couldn't mistake the sound. Or the smell. It stank – of drains and rubbish and muck. She struggled to her feet, feeling the wet starting to penetrate her boots. She found the tunnel wall and pressed herself against it as people pushed past, frantic to get away from the rising tide of filth and terror. Her mind was quite clear and she was surprised to find she wasn't actually frightened. Perhaps there was a point where you got beyond fear. She mustn't get knocked over again, she told herself. She would feel her way along the wall towards the exit and then maybe—

'Don't push now!'

A voice cut across the terrified babble of the crowd. A warm voice with some sort of accent. A voice Rose had heard before.

'Keep calm, ladies and gentlemen, and we will all get out of here in one piece.'

A beam of light came slicing through the darkness, passing over the dark forms of the struggling, stumbling people and lighting up the great wall of water that was gushing from the roof of the tunnel. A beam of light with a figure behind it, a tall, slim figure wearing a tin helmet.

'And please, whoever was singing, carry on!' The figure behind the torch called out again, trying to calm the frantic people as they fought their way towards the exit. The beam of his torch swung through the dust-filled darkness. Rose saw shadows, piles of rubble, terrified faces, mothers clutching their children, an old man falling to the ground—

'Please!' came the voice again. 'Whoever you are! Just keep on singing your song!'

There was nothing at first, just the sounds of rushing water and panicking people. And then:

'*I know where I'm going . . .*'

Rosemary's voice was shaking, making her sound more like Betty than herself, like a little girl who was trying not to cry, but the song already seemed to be calming people down. Their pushing became less frantic, their screams less terrified. And then the beam of the torch found her, standing stock-still as the people surged around her, face white in the darkness, one arm holding Betty clutched close to her side. And as she sang, her voice gained in power, until, by the last line of the song, she was singing with all her might, as loud as she could and with all her heart—

'*The fairest of them all, my handsome, winsome Johnny . . .*'

And then Rose realised: *this* was the moment. The figure behind the torch was Johnny, and Rosemary was looking straight at him.

For a moment they seemed to hang there, the two of them, suspended in time, linked together by the beam of the torch. And then the picture broke up as, with a sickening crack, part of the roof of the tunnel gave way and Rose was hit by a huge wall of water. As she fell, she heard a scream, very close by, and realised with a jolt of surprise that it was her. Everything seemed to slow down. She saw blood on people's faces, hands clutching at the air, Betty screaming as she was knocked down in the rush, Johnny going to help her and being pushed over himself, the torch flying out of his hand and his helmet coming off as he fell, down, down, down on to the tracks where the water was deepest.

And Rose thought: *Is this what happened to Aunt Cosy's long-lost love? Did he die on the northbound platform of Balham underground station?*

And then:

Is that what's going to happen to me?

She thought of Mum and Grandad, and Aunt Cosy sitting in her special chair, and Grace laughing and Ella smirking, and Fred smiling down at her, his eyes all crinkly behind his floppy fringe, and her mind went: *NO!*

There was no way in the world that she was going to let that happen.

She struggled to her feet and fought her way through the desperate, screaming crowd. It wasn't pitch-dark any more, some sort of emergency lighting had come on and was casting a horrible blue light over everything, turning the terrified faces white, making their blood look black. Rose saw Betty on someone's back, being carried towards the exit, but no Rosemary, no Johnny.

Where is she? Where is he?

Where are they?

And then she saw her. Down on the track, up to her knees in water, her hands beneath Johnny's shoulders, trying to lift him out. It was Rosemary.

'Help me!'

Rose knew that was what she said, even though she couldn't hear her amidst the screams of the people and the gushing of the water. She jumped. It wasn't as far down as she expected, but the water still came up to her knees and it was rising, pouring down from the shattered roof in a vile, stinking torrent.

'I'm here!' she shouted. 'I'm coming!'

She waded through the water, shuddering at the smell, until she got to them.

'You take one shoulder,' she yelled. 'I'll take the other.'

Rosemary nodded. Rose's hands ached with cold, but she put them in the water, under Johnny's shoulder. Her eyes met Rosemary's across his still body.

'One. Two. Three—'

One great heave and Johnny's shoulders were up out of the water and on the platform. His legs were easier. They swung them up and then clambered back on to the platform themselves. There was an old man lying face down nearby. Rose didn't want to think what had happened to him.

Johnny was lying on his back, with Rosemary beside him, looking into his face. When she touched his cheek with one finger, his eyes flickered and opened. They focused on Rosemary and for a second the two of them were linked together, just as clearly as they had been by the light from the torch. And—

'Thank you,' he said.

Rosemary looked up at Rose, her face shining in the gloom, as if she'd just had the most wonderful piece of news in the world. And Rose thought, *We did it! We saved him – me and Rosemary saved him! Everything's going to be different now!*

Then a woman pushed past them carrying a crying

child and the picture broke up. Johnny struggled to his feet, coughing with the effort and flinching with pain.

'We need to get these people out of here,' he said, almost to himself. And then, raising his voice to a desperate shout, 'Ladies and gentlemen! Please! Try and stay calm! We—'

There was another crack and the emergency lights went off, plunging them into total darkness. Rose heard the high-pitched scream of a child and Rosemary's desperate shout and she realised that nothing was different. They were still trapped underground, the water was still rising and Rose was falling, down, down, down.

And then, nothing.

9

'Rose? Is that you?'

Rose opened her eyes. She was lying on some sort of camp bed, covered in a rough blanket. There was a face looking down at her, dark eyes shining with amazement and delight.

'Me and Betty have been so scared!'

It was Rosemary. She looked very different from the shocked, white-faced girl Rose had last seen on the platform of Balham station. She looked fresh and pretty and, although her lipstick was as bright as ever, her hair was tucked away under a neat little hat.

'We thought you were—' Rosemary stopped and shook away the thought. 'What happened to you? Where have you *been*?'

'I don't know.' Rose tried to get up. Her body ached all over, her clothes felt stiff and uncomfortable (she was still wearing her parka) and she suspected that she didn't smell very nice. There were other camp beds lined up either side of hers and small wooden chairs against the walls. What was this place?

'What do you mean, you don't know?' Rosemary had bustled away and was clattering about with some tea things that were arranged on a trolley at the other end of the room. Rose could see now that she was wearing some sort of uniform, quite smart, with a jacket and skirt as well as the hat.

'The last thing I remember was Balham station.'

'Balham?' Rosemary stopped clattering to stare at her. 'That was over two months ago!'

Two months ago? So time had moved on again.

'We were lucky to get out.' Rosemary bit her lip then changed the subject. 'I'm in the WVS now!' She indicated her uniform and struck a little pose, then realised from the look on Rose's face that she didn't know what she was talking about. 'Women's Voluntary Service? Serving tea and sympathy to the lost and wounded?'

Rose was still puzzled. 'What date is it now then?' she said.

'It's New Year's Eve!' Rosemary picked up a newspaper that was lying on one of the other camp beds and held it up to Rose. '1940? How come you don't know that?'

There was a photograph on the paper's front page, one that Rose had seen before, when they'd been doing the war at school. It was of St Paul's Cathedral, its dome standing unharmed while everything around it was consumed by smoke and flames.

'What happened that night?' she said. 'The night in Balham, I mean.'

'You don't know that either? They did hush it up, I suppose, didn't want people to know how bad it was.' Rosemary put down the teacup she was holding and took a deep breath. 'Bomb went through the road above the station,' she said. 'Smashed the water main and the sewer.' She shuddered at the memory. 'That was why I took this up.' She indicated her uniform and tried to smile. 'Had to do something, you know? Singing to the people's all very well but . . .'

And then she stopped and just stood there, with a funny little twisted smile on her face.

Rose could tell she was trying not to cry. She got up from the camp bed and went over and put her arms round her, like Mum used to when she was little and she was hurt or upset. Rosemary hid her face in Rose's parka and heaved a great shuddering breath. Rose patted her back, not quite knowing what else to do.

'Oh, Rose, it was so awful.' Rosemary looked up at Rose's face. 'Over sixty people died that night. Sixty! A lot got out, but—' She screwed up her mouth in an effort to stop the tears before she went on. 'I knew some of them, the ones who were—' She stopped, unable to say the word. 'Not terribly well, but still. The lady from the butcher's on the high street, she was ever so nice. A little boy from Betty's school—'

'What about Johnny?' The words came out before Rose could stop them.

Rosemary turned and looked at Rose as if she was seeing her for the first time. She seemed unable to speak.

'The boy we saved from the water?' said Rose. 'Did he get out OK?'

But Rosemary didn't answer. 'Johnny . . .' she repeated the name carefully as if it was something precious. 'Is that his name?' She smiled to herself and Rose knew she was picturing his face. 'It suits him.'

Rose nodded. 'Like in your song.'

Their eyes met and the same smile crept across both

their faces.

'Do you know what happened to him, Rosemary?'

Rosemary forced herself back into the present with a little shake. 'They took him away,' she said. 'I don't know where. Hospital, I suppose. He was a hero that night, Rose. If he hadn't arrived, just at that moment, and told me to go on singing like that, many more people would've been—'

'But what about him?' said Rose. 'Do you think he was badly hurt?'

'No! He just got a bump on the head, that's all! Oh gosh, I don't know! I'm never going to see him again, anyway.'

'You don't know that! Rosemary, you've got to—'

'Miss Miles!'

An older woman had come in, her footsteps ringing busily on the wooden floor. She was wearing the same uniform as Rosemary and leading a younger woman with a white face whose right arm hung loose and helpless beneath her coat. A little boy with dirty knees was trailing along behind them, kicking at the floor and dragging his feet.

Rosemary jumped to attention. 'Sorry, Mrs Pinker!'

'Tea, please! Lots of sugar!' called the woman. She had the kind of accent Rose remembered from the old British films she used to watch on television with Grandad on a Sunday afternoon. War films, they were mostly, but sometimes not. There was one called *Brief Encounter* which Rose had loved, full of trains and smoke and sadness. 'And cocoa!' added the woman, and turned to the boy. 'That all right, young man?'

While Rosemary prepared the drinks, Rose looked around. The room felt somehow familiar, with its high windows and its smell of chalk and powder paint, damp clothes and unwashed hair. It was a smell that stirred all sorts of half forgotten memories in the depths of Rose's brain . . . It was . . . it was . . .

Of course! It was the smell of a primary school. They were in a disused primary school, which obviously hadn't been disused for very long. You could still see the marks on the walls where the children's pictures had been pinned up and there were some old-fashioned desks with ink stains and hinged lids shoved away in one corner.

'Miss Miles! What has happened to those drinks?' The older woman was getting impatient.

'Coming, Mrs Pinker!'

Rosemary hurried over with two steaming mugs, leaving Rose by the trolley, breathing in the smell of the children whose presence still hung about the old classroom like mist. She'd gone to a primary school like this, one of the old ones, built of red brick. She remembered the big iron radiators and the gritty, grey playground that hurt your knees when you fell over. In fact, this might even be the primary school she went to. She looked around, imagining herself sitting there with Grace and Ella, giggling and pinching each other while Mrs Lavis talked about long division and spelling and the Romans.

'Are we still in Balham?' she said as Rosemary came back.

'What? Of course we're still in Balham!' Rosemary picked up a teaspoon and examined her reflection in it as if it was a tiny hand mirror. 'Where else would we be?'

So it *was* her old school. Rose felt stupid tears prick her eyes. 'I'm sorry. I know it sounds weird.'

Rosemary sighed and put down the teaspoon. 'No. I'm sorry. I'm tired. Listen. My shift finishes in a tick. Why don't you come back with me?'

'Back?'

'Home. Nightingale Lane. Mother won't mind and Betty would love it. She hasn't stopped talking about you since that night when you followed us home from the tube. She thinks you're an angel sent to look after us.'

Rose hesitated. 'I don't know . . .'

'Oh, come on!' Rosemary grabbed her arm and started bustling her over to the door. 'What else are you going to do? You can't stay here for ever. Cheerio, Mrs Pinker! See you Thursday!'

Mrs Pinker was bandaging the woman's arm. She looked up and nodded as Rosemary and Rose went out into the icy brightness of the school playground. Everything was sparkling with frost. The clean icy smell reminded Rose of the last days of the autumn term, full of rehearsals and carols and parents coming into school.

'It smells like Christmas,' she said.

Rosemary breathed in the smell as they started to walk. 'It does, doesn't it? Wasn't much of a Christmas for poor old Bets this year. No turkey, no crackers, no pud. Hardly any presents to speak of. Lucky she had your dog.'

Of course. Tommy was there, looking after Betty. Rose suddenly wanted to see him very much.

'How is he?' she said.

Rosemary grinned. 'See for yourself!' She nodded at the road ahead as they turned the corner into Nightingale Lane.

A bundle of black-and-white hairiness, skinny legs and wagging tail was flying along the pavement towards them in a great scrabble of claws and happiness. It was him. It was Rose's Tommy.

'Hello, hairy.' She crouched down and buried her face in his fur, breathing in his dry doggy smell and trying not to cry.

'Coseeeeeee!' Betty came pounding up the pavement towards them, arms outstretched and plaits flying. She hugged her sister's legs. 'You're back! And you've found the strange girl again!' She looked up at Rosemary. 'Is she coming home with us? To help look after Tommy?'

Rosemary grinned. 'What do you think, Strange Girl? Are we taking you home?'

Rose looked up at them, the big sister and the little one who was now swinging off her sister's legs as if she was a lamp post. She'd normally be embarrassed, find some excuse, if someone she didn't really know asked her something like that. But this was different. This was her family. And there was a war on. So she nodded.

'Yes,' she said. 'Thank you. I'd like to come home.'

10

'So you never saw him again?'

Rose was sitting on the bed in her old room at the back of the house in Nightingale Lane with Tommy at her feet. Except it wasn't her room now. It was Rosemary's. It didn't look all that different actually. Instead of the stripped wooden floorboards, there was a sort of brown-ish lino on the floor, a bit worn in places, and a different cover on the bed, a faded thing printed with pinkish flowers. The old fireplace was still there, though, and the bed was in exactly the same place, along the wall opposite the window. Even the coldness of the white china doorknob in Rose's hand had felt familiar.

'After that night in Balham? No.'

Rosemary was getting changed. She'd taken off the heavy grey uniform she'd been wearing at the rescue centre and was now wearing a scratchy-looking old dressing gown over her slip while she rummaged about inside an unfamiliar dark wardrobe.

'Brrr!' Rosemary shivered. The room was chilly, in

spite of the two bars of the electric fire that glowed red and made the room smell of electricity and hot dust.

'But you think he was taken to a hospital?' said Rose. 'Did you never try and find out which one?' *It was so difficult to find someone,* she thought, *without phones and the internet and everything. How did anyone ever get to meet anybody more than once?*

Rose stopped clattering about with coat hangers and swung round, holding a scarlet dress on a hanger in front of her like a shield. 'No!' She sounded outraged at the idea. 'What do you think I am? We only met once! I'm not going chasing all over London looking for some boy, just because—'She stopped and bit her lip. They both knew what she had been going to say.

'Because what?'

Rosemary shook away the words that hung in the air between them and turned back to the wardrobe.

'Because you fell in love with him?' The words tumbled out before Rose could stop them. She'd never said anything like that before, not even to her best friends. They'd never talked about those sorts of things, she and Grace and Ella. They talked about boys, of course they did. But it was just jokes and teasing and the occasional bit of crying on each other's shoulders when things went wrong or got particularly embarrassing. They didn't talk about 'love'. And if they had they would've called it 'lurve', to show they didn't really mean it.

Rosemary didn't seem embarrassed. She turned away from the wardrobe and looked at Rose, still holding the red dress against her chest.

'You're right,' she said. 'I suppose I did. I didn't know it was that at the time, though. He just seemed . . . familiar. Do you understand?'

Rose nodded. She understood very well. It was how she'd felt when she'd first met Fred. Did that mean . . . *that he was her Johnny*? The thought made her feel scared and happy at the same time. And then she remembered the message she'd sent him and told herself there was no point in thinking about him any more. It was over. He was miles and miles and years and years away and she was probably never going to hear from him again. She looked at Rosemary who was still posing in front of the mirror with the red dress.

'What are you going to do?' she said.

Rosemary put the dress on the bed and went over to sit at the dressing table. It was under the window, where Rose had her desk, and was one of the old-fashioned ones with three mirrors at different angles, so you got three different reflections of yourself. Aunt Cosy had one like it in her room at home. Perhaps it was the same one. Rose wondered when her aunt had changed bedrooms. Maybe when she was grown-up and her mum had died?

'I don't know,' she said. Three Rosemarys looked out at Rose from the mirrors. 'People are losing people all the time. Really losing them, I mean. It feels silly to care so much about a boy I don't even know.'

'You mustn't give up.' Rose thought of her ninety-two-year-old aunt looking at the photograph in her memory box. *One that got away, sweetheart. One that got away.* 'If you do, you might regret it all your life.'

'Perhaps.' Rosemary stared at her own reflection for a second, looking so much like her older self that Rose felt her skin prickle. Then, shaking the moment away, 'There's a dance tonight,' she said, turning to Rose with a grin. 'A big one, for the New Year, at Covent Garden. You know, the opera house? Billy's playing, with his band. He's been on at me to go.'

Rose stared at her. 'But – I thought you said the bombers always come at night now?'

'They do.' Rosemary turned back to the mirror and started to fluff up her hair. 'What's that got to do with anything?'

'Well – is it safe? To go out, I mean?'

Rosemary shrugged. 'You're not safe anywhere these days, not really, out or in. But we've got to keep on going, haven't we? No matter how bad things get. Just put one foot in front of the other and keep on going. That's what Mr Churchill says, anyway.' She put down her hairbrush. 'I wasn't going to go,' she went on. 'Didn't want to give Billy the wrong idea. But'– she put her head on one side and looked at Rose from out of the mirror – 'if *you* came . . .'

'What? Oh no. I don't think so. I can't dance.'

'You don't have to. I couldn't go on my own, Rose. But with you, it'd be different. Come on, we deserve to have some fun. Mother will be back from her shift soon, she can look after Betty.'

Rose shook her head. 'Look at me.' She indicated her filthy, twenty-first-century clothes. 'I can't go to a dance like this.'

Rosemary looked her up and down. 'Hm. Not exactly glam, are you?' Then, 'I'll lend you something!' She jumped up from her chair and started to clatter about in the wardrobe again. 'Here!' She brought out a plain dress, dark-blue with long sleeves and tiny black buttons down the front. 'This will suit you. Get up, come on, get up on your feet, your country needs you!'

Rose couldn't help laughing as she got up. Rosemary held the dress up against her and together they looked at her reflection in the long mirror on the wardrobe door.

'You see! It does suit you!'

Rose wasn't sure. 'It's a bit . . . *lady-ish*,' she said. This was one of Grace's invented words and was what they used to describe anything too smart, too feminine, too like something a *teacher* would wear.

'Lady what? Ish? Is that a bad thing?'

Rose shrugged. 'Maybe?'

'It's fine.' Rosemary had decided. She threw the dress down on the bed next to the red one. 'Now, shoes! Your feet are bigger than mine.' She stretched out one leg and admired her toes. 'Mother!' she said suddenly. 'She must be about your size. Stay!' she added, pointing one finger at Rose. Tommy looked up, puzzled, before he realised she wasn't talking to him. Rosemary was at the door now. 'And put on the dress!' She shot out of the room, banging the door and leaving a deep silence behind her.

Rose smiled and scratched Tommy's head. She'd forgotten how much fun it was, getting ready to go out. She and Grace and Ella used to spend hours round each other's houses, trying on clothes and deciding what to wear. That was before all the wedding stuff had started, of course. There was no point in getting dressed up when you didn't go out any more.

She heard Rosemary arguing with Betty out on the landing, so she quickly took off her jeans and her top and wriggled into the dark-blue dress. It was difficult at first and at one point there was a nasty ripping sound, but then Rose discovered a zip at the side. This made things easier. She pulled the dress over her head and wriggled her arms into the sleeves. Then she looked in the mirror.

Rosemary was right. The dress did suit her. The dark-blue looked good against her pale face and made you notice the colour of her eyes.

'Look look look!' Rosemary burst back into the room, brandishing a pair of shoes. 'These will fit you, I know they will, I can feel it in my bones!'

The shoes were neat black lace-ups with a small heel. They were nothing like anything Rose would wear normally, but they fitted and, unlike her boots, they didn't smell. She put them on and together she and Rosemary looked at her reflection again.

'Hm,' said Rosemary. 'You need something. I know!' She went over to the dressing table and scrabbled about among the pots and jars there. 'Lipstick!' She held up a small gold tube. Rose felt a stab of recognition as she realised it was the one from the memory box.

'Oh, no,' she said, backing away. 'You're not going to put that on me.'

'I am! Believe me, it'll make all the difference. Stay still!' She grabbed Rose's chin in one hand and with the other applied the lipstick, the tip of her tongue protruding from between her own lips as she concentrated. 'There!'

Rose stared at the unfamiliar figure in the mirror. She had never seen herself like that before.

'I look . . . I look . . . *grown-up*,' she said, and watched a slow, delighted, lipsticked smile spread across her face.

'You look beautiful!' Rosemary's face appeared in the mirror beside her. 'Doesn't she, Tommy-dog?'

Tommy wagged his tail and looked from one girl to the other, not understanding, but pleased because they were pleased. Rosemary bent down and planted a kiss on his head.

'You see, Strange Girl?' she said. 'You shall go to the ball!' And she waved an imaginary wand over Rose's head. '*Ting!*'

11

The night was cold and clear and glittering with ice and stars and broken glass. Rose was shivering in spite of her parka, which she was wearing over Rosemary's blue dress. She knew it didn't look right, but who cared? She could take it off when they got there.

'All right, Rose?'

They had come into central London on the tube and Rosemary was leading the way to the opera house at Covent Garden, shining her torch on the pavement in front of them as they picked their way between piles of rubble and broken glass.

'It's so dark.'

'You'll get used to it. Stick close to me and you'll be all right.'

'What happens if there's an air raid?'

'We can go to a shelter, if we feel like it.' Rosemary looked back over her shoulder. Rose saw the gleam of her grin in the dark. 'Or . . . we just keep on dancing!' She looked up at the sky and shook her small fist at an imaginary plane. 'Do your worst, Adolf! London can take it!'

They stumbled on. Rose stood on a piece of glass that crunched under her foot like snow. A dark shape in a doorway turned into a man as a match flared, lighting up his face. He looked at Rose from under his hat, his mouth twisting into a crooked grin, before the flame went out, leaving just the glow of his cigarette in the darkness. There was a cackle of female laughter and a burst of singing from an unseen pub.

'Come on!' Rosemary took Rose's hand and pulled her away. 'Billy said they'd let us in at the stage door. It's this way.'

As they turned into the alleyway, a door flew open and two young women wearing some sort of uniform tumbled out in a gust of laughter and cigarette smoke, then stumbled off into the darkness, their arms round each other. In another doorway a couple were kissing. A black cat scuttled through the beam of Rosemary's torch and somewhere a trumpeter played a few sorrowful notes.

'This is it.'

Rosemary had stopped outside a door in the wall. She shone her torch over chipped green paint and a sign that read 'STAGE DOOR'. As she lifted her fist to knock, the door opened, spilling light into the darkness and revealing the outline of a tall man whose shadow shot out in front of him on to the greasy black pavement.

'Ladies.' He showed them his teeth in a creepy smile and held the door open for them. He was wearing a black suit and bow tie. *One of the musicians?* thought Rose. He looked like a figure from a bad dream.

Rosemary stepped into the light. 'Thank you,' she said, and pulled a 'yuck' face at Rose behind his back as they went through.

Inside, an elderly man in a flat cap was sitting in an ancient armchair, reading the paper in front of an electric bar fire.

'Hello!' Rosemary gave him her biggest smile. 'We're friends of Billy Boyce. He's with the band and he said—'

The man jerked his head down the passageway that led away into the darkness. 'Number eleven,' he said, without looking at them, and went back to his paper.

The walls of the passage were brick and lined with doors that seemed too close together to have rooms behind them. There were sounds of instruments warming up and the occasional burst of smoky male laughter. A door opened suddenly, revealing a man with a small moustache that crawled along his top lip like a caterpillar.

'Good evening, laydeez!' he said without removing the cigarette that was clamped between his teeth.

'We're looking for Billy,' said Rosemary. 'Billy Boyce? Plays the trumpet?'

The man turned back to the room behind him. 'You're in luck, Billy Boy!' he said. 'Visitors!'

Billy's face appeared as the man moved off down the corridor. He looked different from the last time Rose had seen him, smart in his black suit and bow tie. His spots had cleared up too.

'You came!' he said, running a finger round the inside of his collar as he looked at Rosemary. A hot blush spread from his neck up to his face.

'I did, Bill,' said Rosemary. 'And I brought my friend, Rose.'

'So I see.' Billy gave Rose a quick nod and took a drag of his cigarette. 'Look, we're on in a sec, Rosemary, so—'

'Just show us where to go and we'll be out of your hair. Can we leave our coats?'

He nodded again, and when they'd loaded him up with their coats, showed them to the door that took them through to the auditorium.

Rosemary looked at Rose. 'Ready?'

'Ready.'

It was like opening a door into another world. After the scuffed, smoky gloom of the backstage area, the vast auditorium of the opera house shone with gold and glittered with glass and light. The rows of seats at ground level had been taken out and replaced with a dance floor, which was encircled with tier upon tier of balconies rising to the enormous dome of the roof. People were sitting around the edge of the dance floor and in the first balcony, smoking cigarettes and drinking and making each other laugh. It was like fairyland.

Rosemary smiled at Rose's astonished face. 'Like it?' she said.

Rose nodded, unable to speak. She'd been inside old theatres before, to watch pantos at Christmas with Mum and Dad, but she'd never seen one as amazing as this. Then an awful thought hit her like a slap: 'Do we have to dance?' she said. She'd seen the kind of dancing they did during the war and there was no way she'd be able to do it.

Rosemary shrugged. 'If somebody asks us. It would be rude to say no, don't you think?'

This was what Rose had been dreading. 'But I can't. I don't know—'

She was interrupted by a flurry of movement and a murmur of expectation from the crowd. The band was coming on.

'There's Billy!' said Rosemary. 'Look at him with his trumpet, thinks he's everybody. Come on, let's find a good place.'

She led the way across the room as the band started to

play and couples stood up to dance. Most of the men and a lot of the women and girls were in uniform. Rose recognised the khaki of the British Army and the blue of the RAF, but there were others, too, that she couldn't identify, which had to be from different countries. Rosemary stood out in her bright-red dress. They watched as the couples started to move, circling the room as if they were all part of one huge machine.

How did they know how to do that?

Rose was silently praying that nobody would ask her to dance when she realised that someone was already talking to Rosemary. It was a young man, a boy really, with curly dark hair, wearing a navy-blue uniform with wide trousers and a sort of tight-fitting tunic – a sailor, perhaps? Rosemary was laughing and shaking her head, looking over at Rose. The young man shrugged and smiled, then indicated a boy standing behind him, who was wearing the same uniform. Rosemary looked at Rose and grinned: *Shall we?*

No, thought Rose, trying to communicate with Rosemary through her eyes. *Please! Nonononono!*

But it was too late. The dark-haired boy had whisked Rosemary away and they were disappearing into the crowd. She saw Rosemary's face over her partner's shoulder for one second and then she was gone. Rose was alone. She longed to get out, find the loo, something, anything, but there was no escape. The other boy was smiling at her, pulling a 'what can you do?' face. She couldn't just tell him to go away, could she? As Rosemary said, that would be rude. She thought of all the times she'd been mean to boys, not because she didn't like them or wanted to hurt their feelings, but because she was scared. She didn't want to be like that any more. So she forced herself to smile back at the boy and was amazed to find it wasn't that difficult after all.

He pointed to his chest. 'I. Can. Not. Speak,' he said.

'Oh! I'm really sorry!' Rose was horrified. 'How awful for you.' *Is that all he could say?* she thought. *Has he been injured in the war, perhaps?*

And then she realised he was laughing. 'No!' he said. His teeth were very white against his brown face. 'No no no! I. Can. SPEEE-EEAK . . .'

What?!

He shook his head and pointed to his chest again. 'French!' he said.

'Ohhhh.' It was just that he couldn't speak English! Rose would have been embarrassed but the boy had such a nice face that she laughed instead and pointed to her own chest. 'English!' she said.

He nodded and pointed to himself. 'Ali!' This was becoming a game.

'Rose!' said Rose, doing the same.

This seemed to make him very happy. 'Engleesh!' he said. Rose realised that he wasn't much older than she was. 'Rose!' he repeated. 'Engleesh Rose! *C'est parfait!*' And he held out his hand. Rose took it and he whirled her away into the crowd.

And it was fine, actually, much easier than she'd expected. Grandad had tried to teach her to waltz once, at a wedding reception when she was little. But she'd never got the hang of it. He'd put her off with all his 'ONE-two-three, ONE-two-three's and his 'Come on, Cabbage, you can do it, keep up!' and then she'd stood on his bad foot and they'd had to stop.

But this was different. It was as if the music was controlling her feet – or maybe just that Ali was a better dancer than Grandad. Rose seemed to float around the room in the whirl of people and the speckles of light thrown by the giant mirror ball that hung from the ceiling, conscious only of Ali's hand on her back and her hand in his hand and the smell of sweat and cigarettes and perfume and happiness. And a thought dropped into her brain—

I'm happy, it said. *I, Rose, am happy.*

You don't usually notice it at the time, she decided. You might think afterwards: *That was a lovely afternoon. I was really happy then.* But you don't when it's happening. You're too busy being happy. But this time, she did notice and she was glad. She decided that she'd try and notice more often.

And then the number had finished and everyone was clapping. Rosemary appeared at her elbow.

'See?' she said. 'I told you it'd be fun!' And then she looked at the stage and her face dropped. 'Uh-oh,' she said. 'What's he up to now?'

Billy had made his way to the front of the stage, trumpet in one hand, looking self-conscious and important. He cleared his throat into a microphone.

'Ladies and gentlemen,' he said. 'I'm sorry to announce that our usual singer can't be with us tonight.'

There were a few groans and shouts of 'shame!'

'But!' Billy held up his hand to silence them. 'We are lucky to have with us in the audience a friend of mine who might just be persuaded to take her place.'

A murmur of interest ran through the crowd. Rose looked at Rosemary. She had her eyes shut like a little girl who was pretending she wasn't there.

'Rosemary?' Rose hissed. 'Does he mean—'

Rosemary screwed up her face even tighter and shook her head.

'She's been down in the shelters singing to the people since the start of the Blitz,' Billy was saying, 'so I think

92

we can persuade her to join us onstage for a number tonight.'

'*Rosemary?*' Rose said again. She had never thought her brilliant, extrovert friend would be nervous about going onstage.

'I can't,' said Rosemary. She still had her eyes shut. 'Not here, not now. *Not with a band.*'

A spotlight was swinging over the upturned faces of the crowd, searching for her. As Rose looked up, she saw its beam brush past a tiny upright figure in a silky blue dressing gown, watching from the top balcony. So Aunt Cosy was here. She gave Rose a little wave, and blew a kiss from the end of her finger. Rose blew it back, then turned to Rosemary. Everything had become very clear.

'Rosemary,' she said. 'You must.' She didn't understand why, but she knew it was very important that the girl who was to become Aunt Cosy got up onstage and sang tonight.

Rosemary opened her eyes and looked at her, astonished. She had never heard Rose so determined before. Neither had Rose, actually.

'If you can sing in an underground station that's been hit by a bomb, you can sing with a band.' Rose grabbed Rosemary's hand in case she decided to make a run for it. 'You can, Rosemary,' she said. 'You know you can.'

Rosemary opened her mouth to object, but it was too late. The spotlight had found her. As it lit up her face it was as if another light went on inside her and she became a different person from the frightened girl she'd been a moment before. She looked surprised for a second and then smiled as if to say 'What, me?', before starting to make her way through the crowd towards the stage, turning only to stick her tongue out at Rose over her shoulder. When she reached the front, Rosemary took Billy's

93

outstretched hand and he helped her up the three steps on to the stage. She whispered something to him. He nodded and spoke to the band leader. Then slowly, very slowly, Rosemary turned and faced the crowd. There was an expectant hush as someone slid the microphone stand in front of her. And then she started to sing.

'*I'll be seeing you, in all the old familiar places . . .*'

The piano joined in with her first, following her as she sang. She was in charge.

'*That this heart of mine embraces . . .*'

Her voice was sweet but husky, different from the clear sound when she had sung the other song.

'*All day through . . .*'

As the rest of the band joined in, Rose realised the French boy was still there, next to her. He smiled and took her hand, then turned back to watching Rosemary. Everyone was watching Rosemary.

'*I'll find you in the morning sun . . .*'

And then she stopped. The musicians exchanged looks. The spotlight continued to sweep over the heads of the crowd. Rosemary started again.

'*I'll find you in the morning sun . . .*'

She faltered again as she looked out into the audience. And then Rose realised. Rosemary had seen a face in the crowd. A face that she knew. The face that she had been waiting to see again.

'*And when the night is new . . .*'

Rose stood on her toes and tried to see over the heads of the people. Where was he? Where was he? Where—

'*I'll be looking at the moon . . .*'

Rose squeezed the French boy's hand and then let it go, so she could move to a better position to see who it was that Rosemary was singing to.

'*But I'll be seeing you . . .*'

Rosemary had come out from behind the microphone now and was making her way down the steps into the crowd. And Rose saw. She'd known who it was all along, whose face Rosemary had seen out there, the boy that she was singing to. This was why Aunt Cosy was there. This was what she wanted Rose to see.

The crowd parted in front of Rosemary as she walked across the dance floor, never taking her eyes from his face, the face that was now lit up by the spotlight and was looking straight back at her.

Johnny.

Rosemary took his hand, and, as the band took up the melody again, they began to dance.

12

After a few more dances with Ali, Rose had danced with an English soldier who looked about fourteen and asked her if she'd ever been to Manchester. Then there was a boy with very light-blue eyes who couldn't speak any English at all who she thought might be Polish, then an Australian who trod on her feet and made her laugh and told her he was from a place called Wangaratta, and a Nigerian with sad eyes who told her all about his girlfriend back home, and then Ali again. They hadn't all danced as well as him but Rose didn't care. She'd forgotten everything as she whirled around the dance floor – her dad, Fred, Mum's wedding day, the row with Grandad. The fact that she was stuck in the wartime London of her aunt's memory and had no idea how she was going to get back. None of it mattered any more. There was just her and the music and the lights.

And Rosemary? Rosemary had just danced with Johnny. And when the band had stopped playing and everyone had counted down to midnight and cheered and kissed and hugged with a kind of desperate intensity because they knew they might never see each other again, and Ali had kissed Rose's hand, Rosemary and Johnny had just stood there looking at each other, a still point in the heart of all the whirling excitement.

And then it was over. It was 1941. The band started packing up and people drifted away. Rosemary kissed Johnny's cheek and he stayed quite still in the middle of the dance floor and watched her as she ran over to Rose in a glitter of joy and they made their way to pick up their coats. They went back though the door by the stage, leaving the shining splendour of the dance hall for the dingy backstage muddle of beer bottles and cigarette smoke and musicians, laughing and saying their good-byes before the journey home.

'Happy New Year, mate, good luck!'

'Goodnight, good luck!'

Nobody knew what they'd have to face on the way home. Nobody knew what they might find when they got there. Rose hoped it was going to be a happy new year for them all, but she didn't think it would be. The Blitz wasn't over, not yet, she remembered that much from History at school and what Grandad had told her – the war would go on for another four years and many more people – millions – would be killed, maybe some of the people she'd met. Some of the boys she'd danced with tonight . . .

'Rose! Are you coming with us or not?'

Rosemary had found their coats and they stumbled out together into the night. Billy trailed along behind them with his trumpet case as they groped their way through the twinkling darkness to the tube station, avoiding the stumbling drunks and kissing couples. Neither of them said anything. They didn't need to. They both knew that something had happened tonight.

And now they were on their way home, feeling lucky to have found a seat in the crowded train. There was a group of Scottish soldiers in kilts standing nearby who swayed and laughed every time the train lurched round a corner. Two young women in khaki uniforms were fast asleep on the seat opposite, their heads on each other's shoulders, and a middle-aged couple in evening dress looked on disapprovingly as a young white man in the same uniform as Ali, but wearing a hat with a red pom-pom, sang something in French.

'*Sur le pont d'Avignon—*' he sang.

'Whoaaah!' went the Scottish soldiers as the train swayed.

Billy was standing in the aisle, his trumpet case in one hand, staring at nothing, and Rosemary was quiet, glowing with a sort of shining happiness. It was Rose who wanted to talk.

'What did he say?' she asked. 'Rosemary! Are you going to see him again?'

Rose turned her gaze on Rose, as if she was surprised to see her. 'What?'

'Johnny . . . !' said Rose. For a brief second she wondered why Billy's mouth twisted in an ugly way when she said the name but she was too keen to hear Rosemary's news to think about it for long. 'Have you arranged to meet?'

'Oh!' said Rosemary. 'Yes.' She nodded to herself as if she had only just remembered. 'Yes, we have. We said tomorrow. I mean, today.'

'New Year's Day.'

Rosemary nodded, stretching out her feet in front of

her and smiling at her shoes. 'Twelve o'clock. At the bandstand on the common.'

I've done it, thought Rose. *I've helped reunite Aunt Cosy with her lost love. Everything's going to be different now – they'll get married and live happily ever after and Aunt Cosy won't spend her life alone. And if that was the point of her bringing me here, then maybe, just maybe, it means we can both go home . . .*

She didn't feel so bad about the wedding now. It was like Aunt Cosy said, Mum had to grab her chance of happiness with both hands and hang on to it for dear life. Rose knew that now. It was just a shame that she'd blown her own chance when she sent that message to Fred . . .

But she wasn't going to think about that now. 'Where's he from?' she said. 'He's not a Londoner, is he?'

'British Guiana.' Rosemary pronounced the name carefully.

'Where is that? Part of Africa?'

Rosemary shook her head. 'South America. He came over with a bunch of others. To help us fight the Nazis.'

'So he's a warden, like Billy?'

Billy's mouth twisted again at the mention of his own name. Rosemary shook her head again.

'Fire service, stationed in Soho.'

'He's right in the middle of things then.'

Rosemary nodded. 'But he's applied to join the RAF, now they've dropped the colour bar.'

'*Colour bar?*' Rose looked at her. 'Does that mean what I think it does?'

'Mm?' Rosemary smiled at her vaguely. 'I don't know. I think you used to have to be what they called "of pure European descent" or something. Silly.'

Rose couldn't believe she was so casual about it. 'It's not *silly*! It's disgusting! Especially when you think

99

about what they're fighting against!'

Rosemary shrugged. 'They've changed it now.'

'Only because they need more people to fight!'

'Johnny wants to be a pilot.' Rosemary smiled and Rose felt her anger melt away. She knew Rosemary was thinking about how handsome Johnny would look in the blue-grey uniform of the RAF. She thought back to the newspaper cutting in Aunt Cosy's memory box. It was an RAF uniform Johnny was wearing in the photo, she realised. So he'd got his wish and became an airman. But maybe that wouldn't happen now. Maybe now she'd helped bring them together, Johnny would stay in London to be with Rosemary? Maybe she had changed the course of history . . .

The train rattled on, past the stations she knew so well. The windows were covered in a sort of mesh, but you could see where you were when the doors hissed open and people stumbled off and on: Embankment, Waterloo, Kennington . . .the familiar names made Rose feel safe. It was still the same old London, whatever century she was in. It was still home.

'Are you all right, Billy?' Rose surprised herself by starting a conversation. She was usually shy with people she didn't know very well (particularly boys), worried that she wouldn't be able to think of anything to say. But she felt sorry for Billy as he stood there staring at the blacked-out windows, his face white and greasy-looking in the blue lights in the carriage, his eyes red and blood-shot as if he'd been crying. Billy didn't reply.

'*Sur le pont d'Avignon* . . .' sang the French sailor.

'Whoaaah!' went the Scottish soldiers.

Rose tried again. 'The band was good,' she said and then felt silly for saying something so obvious. 'How long have you been playing the trumpet?'

'Long enough,' he said, without looking at her.

Oval . . . Stockwell . . . Clapham North . . .

'*L'on y danse, l'on y danse . . .*' sang the sailor.

'Shh! Shh! Shh!' The Scottish soldiers were tiptoeing past the sleeping girls. One big man with fair hair stopped and looked down at them.

'Ahh! Aren't they sweet?'

'*SHHHHHH!*'

Clapham Common. The soldiers tumbled out on to the platform and the French sailor sat down and stared at the sleeping girls, before falling asleep himself.

'Next stop,' said Rose. Then, 'Do you think Betty will be awake when we get in?' She hoped she would be. She was looking forward to watching her face while Rosemary told her about their evening.

'Oh yes!' said Rosemary. 'She'll be awake all right. Mother won't have been able to get her to sleep. She was on at me to let her come, you know, when you were getting changed.'

'What, Betty?' said Rose. 'She wanted to come to the dance?'

'Oh, she always wants to come to everything. "When you're a big girl, Betty," I said, "you can go to all the dances you want, you can dance the night away in cities all over the world, because the war will be over and you will be a grown-up lady with lipstick and earrings and a beautiful red dress like your sister. But for now, you've got to stay at home and look after Mummy."'

Rose laughed. 'What did she say?'

'She said it wasn't fair and Munk-munk thought I was a stinker.' Rosemary shook her curls and laughed as the train rattled to a halt. Clapham South. The doors sighed open and she got to her feet.

'Are you coming, Billy Boyce?' she said. 'Or are you

going to stay on this train all night twiddling your thumbs?'

He turned to look at her, his mouth a thin, straight line. 'That colour bar was there for a reason,' he said as he followed them off the train.

Rosemary and Rose both stopped dead in the middle of the platform.

'What?' said Rosemary, turning to glare at him.

'*What?!*' said Rose.

Billy's eyes flicked nervously. 'Well, they're not British, are they?' he said. 'Africans, people like that. Infantry is all very well for their sort. But the RAF?'

Rose felt her cheeks get hot with fury, but Rosemary was icily calm.

'For your information, *Billy*,' she said, spitting out his name as if it disgusted her, 'Johnny is not African, he is from *British Guiana*. But even if he was, it would make no difference. *You* would still be an ignorant little blighter and *he* would still be a thousand times the man you'll ever be. Rose?'

Rose took the arm Rosemary offered and they stalked off together to the creaky wooden escalator that carried them up to the ticket hall. It was only when they reached the top and were sure Billy was out of earshot that they dared to look at each other and exploded into giggles.

'Whoah!' said Rose. 'You told him!'

'I did, didn't I?' Night, Albert!' Rosemary threw one of her smiles at the old man who was checking tickets. She seemed to know everybody. 'Happy New Year!'

'Goodnight, sweetheart,' he said. 'Stay lucky.'

Rosemary blew him a kiss from the tip of her finger and took Rose's arm again as they left the station. The night was still and clear and cold and although the searchlights were moving gently over the sky above the

102

common, there was no sound as they set off down Nightingale Lane. It had been a peaceful night in south London.

'*It's a long way to Tipperary, it's a long way to go,*' sang Rosemary, putting a little skip into her step.

Rose joined in, laughing. Rosemary's happiness was catching.

'It's 1941, Rose!' she said as they turned the corner. 'And today I'm going to meet my—'

And then she stopped.

The whole of Nightingale Lane stretched out in front of them into the darkness. There were no street lights, of course, but Rose could make out the silhouettes of the houses at either side of the road and the lamp posts and trees reaching up against the stars. She could also see the dark shape of a vehicle parked halfway along. Two vehicles, their dimmed headlights just visible in the blackout. Voices, giving instructions. A door slamming. Dark shapes moving, men. A woman's voice, raised, anxious, questioning. A stretcher.

A stretcher?

Rose felt a deep thud of dread in the pit of her stomach.

Rosemary said, 'Betty.'

And she started to run.

13

'Rose. Tell Johnny.'

Rosemary's face was white in the darkness. A woman who had to be her mum was getting into the back of the ambulance. Rose couldn't see her face. She didn't want to. She looked at Rosemary instead. 'I will, Rosemary. I promise.'

And so it had happened. While they were dancing at Covent Garden, Betty had been hurt, badly by the look of it. Rose had just caught a glimpse of her little face above the white nightdress as they put the stretcher into the ambulance. Her eyes were closed.

She had been dancing in the garden, the man had said, the warden who had come when her mum had gone screaming out into the road. There'd been no heavy bombing in the area that night but the sky had been alight with incendiaries and flares and gunfire from the common as a squadron of bombers passed over. It was like a firework display, he said. *Or a ballroom with a mirror ball twirling*, Rose had thought, feeling sick as she remembered the vision she'd seen from her bedroom window. It was a piece of shrapnel, perhaps, the warden said, from one of our guns even, a chance in a million, she didn't feel it, almost certainly didn't even know—

'*That does not help!*' Rosemary had shouted in his face. The man had looked away. And now:

'Rose?'

'I promise,' Rose repeated. 'You go. Just go. I'll be all right.'

Rosemary held out her hand. As Rose took it, Rosemary's face crumpled for a second, but she didn't cry. She squeezed Rose's hand and then turned away and got into the back of the ambulance. Rose watched it drive away into the darkness.

'You'll be all right, love?' The warden looked too tired to care much. His face was grey with dust and sorrow. He had other people to look after, other bad news to share.

Rose nodded. The front door had been left open and she could see Tommy waiting for her in the hall. As the warden got into his van she saw Billy Boyce watching from across the road. Their eyes locked for a moment and then he turned and walked off into the darkness carrying his trumpet case. Good riddance.

Rose closed the door on the night and buried her face in Tommy's fur. She didn't think she could bear this without him.

'What are we going to do, Tom?'

The cuckoo clock on the wall had stopped at ten minutes to midnight. *Was this when Betty was . . . hurt?* Rose wondered. She hadn't even been able to see the New Year. *But she'll be all right*, she told herself. *They'll take her to hospital, where they'll look after her. She'll probably be out in a few days, and be back to her old self, playing with Tommy and teasing her sister about Billy Boyce.*

Rose went upstairs with Tommy and headed for her old room, Rosemary's room now. She pulled the blue dress off over her head and flopped on to the bed in her underwear, too tired to sleep, to think, to feel . . .

She never knew what woke her. She'd been dreaming that she was chasing Aunt Cosy through endless dark alleys where the air slithered past her like black jelly and her aunt was always disappearing around the next corner, and her heart was pounding with panic and—

She stared into the darkness. Where was she? What was going on?

And then she felt the comforting weight of Tommy on her feet at the end of the bed and smelt the musty dampness of the old house and she realised. She was still there. It was New Year's Day, 1941, and she was still there, lying on Rosemary's bed in her old room in the house on Nightingale Lane.

And she had to be at the bandstand on Clapham Common by twelve o'clock.

She sat up, heart pounding with panic. Tommy looked up from his place at the end of the bed and thumped his tail and she relaxed. *It's all right*, she thought. *It's still dark. There's no hurry, the day hasn't started yet. I can sleep a bit more.*

And then she heard the chirrup of a bird outside and saw the daylight seeping through a gap at the window and remembered the heavy blackout curtains that Rosemary had drawn when they were getting ready to go out and she leapt off the bed and threw open the curtains. Light flooded the room. What was the time?

She ran out on to the landing, downstairs into the hall. The hands of the cuckoo clock hadn't moved from ten minutes to midnight.

What was the time?

And then she heard a voice coming from the front room. It was a man, posh, sounding as if he was lecturing someone, telling them off, like the kind of teacher at school that nobody likes. Someone was in the house.

'Wuff?'

Tommy was at the top of the stairs, looking down at her and wagging his tail. He didn't seem afraid or suspicious. Perhaps there was nothing to be afraid of. Rose took a deep breath.

One. Two. Three—

She opened the door. The room was empty. And the voice said, 'This is the BBC Home Service . . .'

It was the radio. It must have been left on all night, but she hadn't heard it because there were no programmes on until the morning.

'*Here is the news at midday on Wednesday 1st January 1941 . . .*'

Midday? It couldn't be!

Rose took the stairs two at a time, back to Rosemary's room and grabbed her own clothes. They were stiff with mud from the night at Balham station and she had to hold her breath as she pulled her sweatshirt over her head, but at least they were dry. Then she shoved her feet into her boots and her arms into her parka, and started to run.

Down the stairs and out of the house, Tommy behind her, down Nightingale Lane – past the school, the pub where she went for Sunday lunch with Mum and Sal and Leo – round the corner towards the tube station – past the sad sweet shop, its shutters closed against the chilly sunshine – across the road, a bus roaring past, a man shouting 'watch it!' – over the grass . . .

Why was Clapham Common so *big*?

Past the allotments, beyond the trees . . . the big guns in

the distance, the barrage balloons like floating silver elephants . . .

Rose could see the bandstand now, at the end of the path and—

There was nobody there.

Rose climbed up the three steps on to the bandstand and stood there with Tommy, looking at the common stretched out around them, sparkling with frost under the cold white sky.

She could see a man walking a dog, some boys kicking a football over by the trees. There was no sign of Johnny. Perhaps he hadn't arrived yet . . .

But there – sitting on one of the benches near the bandstand, smoking a cigarette – there was a figure she knew.

'Billy?'

He squinted up at her in the sunshine. 'What? Oh, it's you.' He sounded disappointed, but not surprised.

'How long have you been here?' said Rose, hurrying down the steps toward him. *Perhaps he's seen Johnny*, she thought, hope rising in her chest.

Billy made a big deal of looking at his watch, narrowing his eyes as if he was having trouble making out the time. Rose could see that it was now twenty past twelve. Twenty past! How could she have overslept like that? How could she?

'Half an hour or so,' Billy took a drag of his cigarette. 'What of it?'

'Have you seen anyone else?'

He shrugged. 'Couple of old dears out for a stroll. A few kids. Why?'

Rose's heart clenched. 'You didn't see Johnny? The boy Rosemary met last night at the dance?'

Billy shook his head. 'Nope.' He got to his feet and took a last drag of his cigarette, then threw it on the gravel, next to several other dog-ends.

It's not possible, thought Rose. Johnny wouldn't break his date with Rosemary. He must have been here, he must have. Then, an awful thought: *Perhaps he got hurt, caught in a raid on the way home from the dance, perhaps—*

She shook the thought away and grabbed Billy's arm as he started to walk off. 'Are you sure? Billy, this is important!'

Billy stopped and looked down at Rose's hand on the sleeve of his coat and then into her eyes. His pale-blue eyes were bloodshot and his face was close enough for Rose to smell the sour scent of the cigarette on his breath. Tommy growled softly and Rose flinched, but she didn't look away.

'What is it to you anyway?' he said. 'Why do you care so much?'

Tommy growled again.

'I just do.'

'I told you,' he said. 'I saw nobody. Nobody! And I've got better things to do than stand here being interrogated by a kid like you. So if you don't mind . . .'

He shook her hand off his arm and walked away. Rose and Tommy stood there and watched him go.

14

'Can you tell me the way to the nearest hospital?'

The old man at Clapham South station wiped his nose on the sleeve of his jacket and stared at Rose for a long time before replying. 'You looking for someone, love?'

'Yes,' she said. 'My—'

And then she stopped, not knowing what to say. What was Betty to her? She was Aunt Cosy's little sister, so that made her another aunt in a way. But that was too weird. She couldn't say that.

'She's my sister,' she said. 'My little sister.' It felt as if it was true.

'What about your people, love? Mother? Anyone?'

'She's with her,' Rose said. 'She went in the ambulance. I need to find them.' She felt the panic rising in her chest and tears prickling her eyes. 'I don't know where they took her.'

'You could try St Thomas's, that's the most likely.'

'Is that the one by the river?' Rose had been there once to visit Grandad when he was poorly; she and Mum had brought him grapes and a copy of *The Daily Mirror* and he'd made jokes and flirted with the nurses.

The man nodded. 'Do you know how to get there?'

'Yes,' said Rose. 'I think so.'

'You'll need to get a bus,' the man called as she and Tommy turned to go. 'Or the tube!'

But Rose didn't have any money so they set out on foot. They headed north, beyond the common, past boarded-up shops and bomb sites, great craters gaping in the middle of the road, glass everywhere, swept into piles like ice. A house that seemed to have been sliced in half by a giant displayed its rooms with all the furniture intact, the pictures on the walls, sunlight reflecting off a mirror hanging on a bathroom wall. It was like a city in a dream, smoke hanging in the wintry sunshine, burnt wood and brick dust and everywhere that sweet chemical smell of nail varnish remover. People were behaving like they did in dreams too, in strange and unpredictable ways. They passed a woman pushing a dog in a pram and a man who stood in the middle of the road and laughed at nothing. Little boys dodged round them chasing each other with invisible machine guns – BAM-BAM-BAM! BAM-BAM-BAM! – and when they turned a corner into a side street, two men appeared from a ruined house carrying an old-fashioned gramophone between them.

'Fancy a dance, sweetheart?' one of them said without taking his cigarette from his mouth.

Rose shook her head and hurried on, her heart thudding in her ears. As she got to the end of the road she heard the gramophone start up and turned to see that an old woman had come out of her house and was dancing to the music in her apron and slippers.

The damage got worse the closer they came to the centre of the city. An entire street was reduced to heaps of rubble, with just one house standing alone in the middle, like a single tooth in an old man's grin. The house was completely untouched by the destruction around it – its windows were intact and its front garden neat with clipped hedges and snowdrops in bloom. There was even a bottle of milk on the doorstep. Next to it, a group of rescue workers in overalls and tin helmets was working in the ruins of what had been the house next door, digging in the rubble. Rose didn't want to be there to see what they found.

'It can't be far now, Tom. We're getting near the river.' Rose's feet hurt and she felt close to tears, but she wasn't going to admit that; not to herself, not to Tommy. They had to find Rosemary and tell her what had happened. Johnny hadn't been there. He hadn't come as he'd promised. Then they could decide what to do, she and Rosemary together.

The hospital didn't look like the shiny modern one she remembered. It stretched along the south bank of the river, a big, old-fashioned place built of stone, one part of it in ruins where it must have been hit by a bomb. It was very busy, though, far busier than it had been when she and Mum had visited Grandad. Ambulances were lined up along the road and people were coming in and out of the main entrance, nurses with heavy blue capes over their uniforms, women and children, men in boiler suits and tin helmets that Rose now recognised as wardens. But who could she ask? Who would know whether Betty was here?

'Tommy?' He pricked up his ears and gave her his most interested look. 'Tommy, stay!' That wasn't what he wanted to hear, she knew that, but he couldn't come in with her. Dogs weren't allowed in hospitals. He was looking at her as if he didn't understand.

'You'll have to wait here, Tom. Dogs can't—'

But he was gone, shooting off up the steps into the hospital as if he was chasing a squirrel.

'Tommy!' Rose yelled. 'Tommy! Come back!'

She ran after him, into the tiled and echoing space at the top of the steps. Nurses turned and stared at her, people sitting on wooden chairs along the sides of the room looked up with tired faces as Tommy clattered up the big wooden staircase that led up from the entrance hall.

A little boy who'd been waiting with his mum shouted, 'Dog!' and joined in the chase.

'I'm sorry,' Rose said to all the faces turned to her. 'I'll get him. I'm sorry, he's not normally . . .' She gave up trying to explain and ran after him. 'Tommy!'

At the top of the stairs, two porters were wheeling a trolley out of a lift. Tommy ran underneath it, followed by the little boy, but Rose had to dodge around it, being careful not to look at the person who was lying on top.

'Tommy, stop!'

The little boy had skidded to a halt at the feet of a man wearing a white coat. A doctor, judging by the stetho-scope around his neck. Tommy was sitting upright, looking up at the man's face as if he was expecting a treat.

'Whoah!' said the doctor. 'What's all this?'

'I'm looking for a girl.' Rose fought to get her breath back. 'Betty. Her name is Betty Miles.'

He looked at her and she realised how silly that sounded. How could one doctor in the whole of this huge hospital know about Betty? She might not even be here. They might have taken her to any hospital in London, not just the nearest.

'She's a little girl,' said Rose. She took a deep breath, feeling the tears bubbling up behind her eyes. 'Her mum and her sister will be with her?'

The doctor shook his head. Rose tried again.

'She was brought in during the night? Injured?'

'Have you checked the casualty department?' he said. 'If she was injured—'

A woman had stopped beside them, a nurse. She put a hand on the doctor's arm.

'Betty?' she said, looking at Rose. 'Elizabeth Miles? Five years old?'

Rose's heart lifted with hope. And then she saw the look that passed between them, the doctor's face with a question, the nurse replying with a tiny shake of her head. They both looked at Rose.

'I'm so sorry,' said the nurse.

Rose stared at her face. It seemed unnaturally clear against the background of the corridor which had become misty and out of focus. She bit her lip so hard it started to bleed. That was why her aunt never talked about her little sister, the one who had first called her Cosy. She had been killed in the war. When she was only five.

'Where are they?' she said. 'Betty's mum, I mean, and her sister? Can I see them?'

'I think they left,' said the nurse. 'I remember the sister saying she was going to take her mum out of town for a while, to relatives in the country. I expect you'll know . . . ?'

Rose didn't know. How could she? She backed away.

'I'm really very sorry,' said the nurse again. 'Will you be—'

'It's fine,' said Rose. It wasn't, of course, but what could she say? 'I'm fine,' she said.

The nurse and the doctor shared another look and then

moved off in separate directions, leaving Rose and Tommy in the corridor. They had other patients to look after, she knew that. To them, Betty was just one little girl among thousands of others who would never grow up to dance the night away in every city in the world and wear lipstick and earrings and a beautiful red dress like her sister.

Rose didn't know how long she stood there in that chilly corridor, trying not to cry. People walked round her, nurses and doctors and porters with patients on trolleys and in wheelchairs. Some of them looked at her curiously, but none of them stopped. Betty was gone, and Johnny and Rosemary were separated for ever. And now Rosemary had left London, leaving Rose trapped there, alone in the web of her aunt's memories. Where was Aunt Cosy? Why had she brought her here and then disappeared?

And what was Rose supposed to do now?

15

They walked in the thickening dusk, back through the ruined streets of the shattered city, all the way back to the house on Nightingale Lane. Rose didn't know what else to do.

It was getting dark by the time they arrived and although the front door was locked (in her hurry to get to the common that morning, Rose must have slammed it behind them), the back door had been left open and was banging in the wind. The door of the Andersen shelter was open too, the doorway gaping like a toothless mouth at the end of the garden. It was very cold.

'Come on, Tom. In we go.'

As she followed Tommy indoors, Rose realised she hadn't been in the kitchen since Betty's accident. It didn't look any different, not really. There was the same clutter of saucepans over the cooker, the big brown teapot on the draining board, the greyish dishcloth hanging over the tap . . . but it felt like everything had changed. The air seemed to hum with the terror and pain of that moment, the moment that Betty's mother knew that something terrible had happened to her little girl. Rose looked at the half finished cup of tea on the kitchen table, the spilled sugar, the chair knocked over on the floor and thought, *This must have been where she was sitting. Where she was sitting when she heard . . .*

She couldn't bear to think about what Betty's mum had heard, so she pushed the thought away and made herself remember what Rosemary had said: 'We've got to keep on going, haven't we? No matter how bad things get. Just put one foot in front of the other and keep on going.' She picked up a grain of sugar on the end of her finger and licked it off, then found a tin bowl and gave Tommy a drink of water.

But she couldn't bear to stay in that kitchen a moment longer. The radio was still on in the front room, talking to nobody, so she went through.

She hadn't really looked at the room till now, not properly. It was familiar but not familiar. Aunt Cosy's special chair was in its place by the fire, and although it was covered in a faded flowery fabric, its same-old shape made Rose feel a bit better. The fire was a little electric thing, like the one in Rosemary's bedroom, but the big gold-framed mirror was there above the fireplace, and the glass-fronted cupboard that held Aunt Cosy's collection of glass paperweights was in the same place in the corner by the window. And there, face down on the rug in front of the fireplace, was Munk-munk.

Rose picked him up. He looked terribly empty without Betty's hand inside him, making his head move and his paw wave, so she slipped him on to her hand.

'Hello, Munk-munk,' she said. He nodded his head to her and they touched noses. Tommy watched, wagging his tail, interested and confused at the same time, and Rose sat down in Aunt Cosy's special chair and closed her eyes.

'Goodnight, children everywhere,' said the voice on the radio. 'Goodnight.'

Bring-bring. Bring-bring. Bring-bring.

Rose was dreaming she was in the house on Nightingale Lane and the phone was ringing but she didn't know where it was. She was running from room to room, opening doors, looking in cupboards, lifting up cushions . . .

And then she was awake, heart pounding and panic roaring in her head. She opened her eyes and waited for the room to come into focus. But it didn't. The room was completely black. And the phone was still ringing. Perhaps it had been ringing all night.

How could this be happening? Did they even have phones in 1941? *Perhaps it's over,* she thought, hope rising in her chest, *perhaps I'm back, back in the twenty-first century.* It was the eleventh of May and her mum was getting married today. There had been no Betty, no Billy, no Johnny. She had never met her Aunt Cosy as a girl and watched her fall in love with a boy she'd never kiss.

And then, as she stared into the particles of tingling darkness and smelled the musty smell of the old house, Rose realised it wasn't over. She was still there, sitting in Aunt Cosy's special chair with Tommy at her feet and Munk-munk on her hand. The war was going on in Europe, bombs were being dropped on London and, in the house on Nightingale Lane, the phone was still ringing.

Rose left Munk-munk on the chair and felt her way through the darkness to the window. When she parted the heavy curtains, she'd been expecting daylight, but instead found herself face to face with the moon. It was just as huge and bright as it had been on the night she'd left, the night she'd followed Aunt Cosy out of the house and down Nightingale Lane, chasing her memories down the escalator of Clapham South underground station. She closed the curtains again and felt around for the light switch. The room sprang into light, making Tommy look up from his place in front of the fireplace.

Bring-bring. Bring-bring. Bring-bring.

Where was that phone? She looked around the room. There was the scuffed floor, the gold-framed mirror over the fireplace, the big old radio . . .

Outside in the hall perhaps. Rose opened the door and the sound leapt into the room, twice as loud as it had been. She looked left, towards the front door where there was a big heap of mail, letters and stuff, piled up on the doormat and spilling across the floor. She picked up one of the letters, hoping to see a date on the postmark or something. It was a brown envelope, a bill by the look of it. Another, with a typewritten address, to Mrs M Miles. That would be Rosemary's mum. She couldn't read the date, and there was no time to think about that now. The phone was still ringing, more insistent than ever, so Rose dropped the letter back with the others and turned away from the door. She saw the phone straight away. It was a heavy-looking black thing with a separate handpiece and a dial, squatting on a little low table by the kitchen door and demanding to be answered. *What a weird place to keep a phone*, she thought as she hurried over.

Bring.

It stopped. Rose turned to see Tommy watching her from the door of the front room and shrugged. Well, what could she do? Whoever had been trying to get through had obviously given up. And then she heard a key in the front door.

Tommy had heard it too. He was standing quite still, watching the door, wagging his tail gently. Rose put her hand on his head.

'Who is it, Tommy? Who's there?'

Whoever was behind the door had got it unlocked now and was struggling to open it, pushing the big heap of mail that was piled against it to one side.

'Oh, botheration . . .' It was a voice Rose recognised.

One more big push and the door was open. It was Rosemary.

She was wearing the dark trousers and jacket Rose had seen her in before, but she looked very different. Her hair and her clothes were grey with dust, there were dark shadows under her eyes and no bright slash of lipstick to brighten her white face. She closed the door behind her and leant against it. And then she saw Rose.

They both stood there for a second, staring at each other, unable to speak. And then Rose held out her arms and Rosemary walked into them and they stood there together in the hallway of the house on Nightingale Lane, faces hidden in each other's hair, while they both pretended not to cry. Then they started talking at once.

'What happened to you?'

'What happened to *you*?'

'I've been walking,' said Rosemary. 'From Victoria station. Couldn't find a bus. It's terrible out there, Rose, a man at the station said it was the worst night so far.'

'But where have you been?'

'Dorking,' said Rosemary. 'Mother's got a sister there, my Aunty Vera. I had to get her away. After . . .'

Rose nodded.

'You know what happened?'

She nodded again.

'So you can see . . .' Rosemary's voice cracked as

she struggled to hold back the tears. 'This house – you know . . .'

Rose did know. The war wasn't halfway over and the house was already too full of memories. Munk-munk was sitting on the chair in the front room and Betty was still outside, dancing in the moonlight.

'But I had to come back,' Rosemary was saying. 'I couldn't stay there, out in the country, with everything that's been going on in London. I would've felt like a coward. This is where I belong.'

And where Johnny is, thought Rose, *unless he's already gone off to join the RAF*. But she didn't say that.

'What about you, Strange Girl?' Rosemary tried to smile. 'What have you been doing since that night?'

'That night?'

'The last time we saw each other, you know. New Year's Eve.'

'How long has it been?'

'What? Well, it's May now, the tenth of May. So that's what, four, five months?'

Five months?

A misty look had come over Rosemary's face. Rose knew she was thinking of Johnny and knew what she was about to ask. 'Rose? Did you—'

Rose shook her head. 'He wasn't there, Rosemary. He didn't come.'

'What?! That's not possible.'

'It's true. I'm really sorry. I was a tiny bit late, but Billy was there and he—'

'*Billy?* What was he doing there?'

They looked at each other and the same thought dropped into their minds.

'Oh no.'

'Oh . . . *no!*'

'He knew, Rosemary.'

'He . . . *knew*!'

'He must have heard you on the train, heard you telling me when you and Johnny were going to meet—'

'And he went there instead, made up some lie, told Johnny I didn't want to see him.' Rosemary stamped her foot, almost like her old self. '*Billy!*'

But before she could say any more the phone started ringing again. Her forehead crinkled in a frown and then she squeezed past Rose to pick up the receiver and—

'*Billy?!*' she said again. 'No, I just got back. I've been with Mother in Surrey.' Her eyes met Rose's. Then: 'I don't care how long you've been trying to get hold of me, Billy. I don't care if you've been ringing all night, every night since New Year's Day. I don't care how sorry you are. *I know what you did!*'

Rose could almost see Billy's white face, the spots on his chin, the Adam's apple moving in his skinny neck as he swallowed and tried to find the words he wanted to say in the face of Rosemary's fury. She kept her eyes fixed on Rose, her mouth set in a straight, determined line.

'Soho,' she said. 'Johnny's post is in Soho.' Then: '*What?!*' Her fist clenched as she listened to Billy's reply. Rose could hear her breath coming faster and faster. What was going on? What was Billy saying? Now Rosemary was talking again. 'Have you got use of a vehicle?' she said. 'A van or something?' She waited for his reply. 'Then come and get us! Right now, Billy! If you really are sorry, if you really want to make up for what you did, *you come and get us right now*!'

Rosemary slammed down the handpiece of the phone and stared at Rose.

'It was like we thought. He told Johnny I'd changed

my mind, that I didn't want to see him after all.'

'Oh, Rosemary . . .'

'I know. Still, he can make up for it now, the little worm.'

'What d'you mean?'

'This raid tonight,' said Rosemary. 'Billy says it's the worst yet. It's not just the East End, it's Piccadilly, it's Westminster, Big Ben, the Houses of Parliament, it's everywhere. Everything's on fire, Rose. It's like they're trying to burn down the whole city.'

'And Johnny's based in Soho? He'll be right in the middle of it.'

Rosemary nodded.

'So what are we going to do?'

'Billy's coming to pick us up. We're going to find him.'

16

'Drive on!' Rosemary had to shout to make Billy hear above the noise of the engine. 'Drive on, drive on, drive on!'

They were getting close to the river now. There were buildings on fire on both sides of the street, warehouses mostly, with shops at ground level, and old brick blocks of offices and flats. Billy's hands on the steering wheel of the old taxi glowed orange in the light of the flames and his pale, greasy face gleamed red, then pink, then yellow as they drove past the fires. His eyes flicked nervously left and right and he licked his lips. There were beads of sweat on his forehead and his upper lip and black smears around his nose. Rose could feel the heat of the fires through the windscreen and the burn of the smoke in her chest and there was the now-familiar, sweet, choking taste in her mouth.

'Where are we going?' she said. She and Rosemary were sitting in the back of the taxi with Tommy on the floor at their feet.

'Westminster.' Rosemary was watching the burning streets pass the windows, her hands clenched in her lap. 'Every fire unit in London's been ordered there.'

'Why? What's so special about Westminster?'

'They're not to let the Abbey burn, that's the orders from the top. Or the Houses of Parliament.'

Billy swerved to avoid a crater in the road. Smoke was pouring from the windows of a block of flats nearby and people with coats over their pyjamas were being helped out of the front door by wardens and rescue workers. Rose saw a mother with a baby in her arms and an old lady holding a birdcage.

Nobody was trying to put out the fire. There were no fire engines to do it.

'But Westminster's not the only area that's being bombed!' Rose felt the anger rising in her chest. 'What about them?' They'd just passed another family on the pavement. An older girl holding a toddler who was nearly as big as her, a little boy clutching his teddy. Their mum was being helped out of the front door by a female rescue worker in a white tin helmet. There was blood on her face. 'What about the people who actually live in this city?'

Rosemary nodded. 'I know.'

'They're protecting empty buildings while the people burn!'

Rosemary nodded again, her eyes still on the burning buildings outside the windows of the cab. 'We're nearly at the bridge,' she said. 'We'll soon be there.'

A fire engine rattled past, bell ringing. Rose was almost embarrassed to find the old nursery rhyme going round in her head.

London's burning, London's burning
Fetch the engines, fetch the engines

Fire fire! Fire fire!
Pour on water, pour on—

Then, a sudden jolt as Billy stopped the taxi.

'Billy?'

He turned to speak to them through the driver's window. 'I'm not going any further,' he said.

What?

Another fire engine rattled past, followed by a taxi pulling some kind of machine on a trailer. Rose and Rosemary looked at each other.

'Billy,' said Rosemary. 'This is your job.'

'It is not,' he said. 'Actually. For your information, I'm a musician, a trumpet player. And when I'm not playing the trumpet, I'm a warden. Not a fireman. My job is to turn up when the fire has been put out and dig people out of the ruins, all right? I do not drive mad girls into the heart of hell. That. Is not. My job. And it's not yours either, come to that.'

'I've got to find Johnny.'

He turned his whole body round in his seat to look at her. '*How?*' he said. 'How are you going to find him? The whole of the north bank of the Thames is on fire. Look at it.'

It was true. Across the river the city glowed orange and red and crimson. Smoke poured up to join the brooding cloud that hung in the air overhead like a bruise that moved and churned and glowed dull pink with the light from the fires.

'I don't know,' Rosemary said. 'But I've got to try.'

Rose could see the Houses of Parliament, silhouetted against the orange glow on the other side of the river, the tower of Big Ben standing upright at the end, its outline blurred by a covering of scaffolding. She understood why Billy was angry. She understood why he was scared. She was too. But Rosemary had other things to think about.

'I'm going to find him, Billy. With you, or without you, I don't care.'

'Without me, then.' He turned away and stared out through the windscreen of the cab. 'There's the bridge. You can walk.'

'You'd let us do that?'

'I couldn't stop you, could I?'

'Thanks,' said Rosemary. 'You really made up for what you did, didn't you, Billy? You drove us all the way to Westminster Bridge and then turned back.'

Billy said nothing. He just carried on staring straight ahead. Rosemary opened the door. She was halfway out of the cab when she turned.

'Rose? You don't have to come if you don't want to.'

Rose looked at her. This was what she had come for – this was why Aunt Cosy had led her into her past, so they could face this together. There was no way she was going to back out now.

'I'm coming,' she said, and slid out of the cab after Rosemary. Outside, she could hear the throb of the planes overhead and a dull roar from the fires across the river.

'You can leave the dog if you want.' Billy's voice came from the front.

Rose couldn't believe her ears. The cheek of him, the cheek.

'What, with *you*?' she said. 'No thanks, Billy. He's better off on the streets. Come on, Tom.'

Tommy jumped out and they started to walk. Rose hadn't quite believed that Billy would leave them there, but he did. As they set out across the road, she heard the taxi's engine start up and looked back over her shoulder to see it swing around, back the way they'd come. Rose walked on, her back stiff with anger. She was filled with so much fury at Billy's cowardice that she had no room left to feel anything else. Rosemary held out her hand.

'All right, Strange Girl?'

Rose nodded. 'Yes,' she said. 'I'm absolutely fine.'

And she was, actually. She took Rosemary's hand and, with Tommy beside them, they set out across the bridge. The river looked like black silk in the moonlight, streaked with orange and red where the flames on the other side were reflected in the water. Billy had been right. The whole of the north bank was on fire. Only the Houses of Parliament and the tower of Big Ben seemed untouched. But there was more to come. Overhead the sky throbbed with the now familiar drone of the bombers.

Where are you? Where are you? Where are you?

They didn't need to ask that any more, Rose thought. *They can see exactly where we are. The whole of London is lit up like a Christmas tree.* She looked up at the planes and for one mad moment felt like waving. 'We're here!' she would call. 'Come and get us!'

And then:

Eeeeeeeeeeeeee!

A horrible tearing sound ripped through the air. It sounded as if the sky was being ripped apart like an old sheet. Then, silence. And:

BOOM.

The bridge shuddered beneath their feet as the bomb hit its target somewhere south of the river. They walked on, another old taxi rattled past them, dragging a trailer. It didn't stop. A plane passed overhead, low enough for its dark shape to block out the stars. Things were whistling down from the sky and splashing into the river on either side of the bridge. Rose didn't know what they were until one fell with a tinny clatter on the road in front of them.

It hissed and started to fizz with greenish-white light, sending out sparks like a firework. That was when Rose realised. It was like the thing that the man in Balham had put out with his helmet.

It was an incendiary bomb.

Rosemary had stopped, unsure of what to do, but Rose felt her fear melt away as all the bottled-up fury of the last hour rose up in her chest. How dare they, how DARE they drop these things on them?

'Hold Tom,' she said to Rosemary, who nodded and bent to grab his collar, all the time watching Rose with big eyes, wondering what she was going to do.

Rose took a step towards the bomb and then, with a mad yell, jumped up with both feet and landed right on top of it. She felt its metal tube collapse beneath her weight and then started to jump up and down, stomping on the sparks and the hissing white light until it hissed no more.

'You did it!' When the last spark was out, Rosemary rushed up and hugged her tightly while Tommy barked at their excitement. 'You did it, Rose! You killed a bomb!'

'I did, didn't I?' Rose felt breathless and giggly. 'Just as well I was wearing my good boots.'

Their eyes met and they collapsed into laughter, standing there on Westminster Bridge while Tommy wagged his tail and London burned around them. Rosemary was the first to pull herself together.

'Come on.'

She held out her hand. Rose took it, but then, when she tried to walk on, she found she couldn't. Her legs refused to move and she realised that she was trembling. Now the anger had left her, she felt the full craziness of what she had just done and what they were about to do. Billy was right. They should have gone back.

'I don't know if I can do this, Rosemary,' she said. 'I really don't.'

Rosemary didn't seem to hear her. She'd stopped quite still and was staring at something at the other end of the bridge. A fire engine rattled past, its bell clanging. 'Look, Rose. *Look!*'

It was Aunt Cosy, her tiny figure silhouetted against the orange glow of the burning buildings. She was standing in the middle of the road and – *she was waving*.

'Who is that, Rose?' said Rosemary. 'Who is that old lady?'

Before Rose could reply, another truck sped past, heading towards the heart of the fires, but Aunt Cosy didn't budge. The truck seemed to pass right through her, and after it had disappeared into the smoke at the other end of the bridge, she'd gone too.

Rose took a deep breath. If Aunt Cosy was here, then Johnny was too. And she and Rosemary were going to find him. She stood up straight, pulled back her shoulders, and this time it was she who held out her hand to her friend.

'Come on,' she said.

Rosemary took her hand and together they set off towards the fire.

17

'You all right, Strange Girl?'

Rose nodded. They'd reached the end of the bridge and were standing at the edge of Parliament Square beneath the tower of Big Ben. Smoke was pouring from nearly every building around the square, and the streets leading off were edged with solid walls of flame. Only the Houses of Parliament and Big Ben's tower, prickly in its scaffolding, were still untouched.

But for how long? thought Rose. *How long?*

She felt hot and cold at the same time. The heat burned her face and the air was full of smoke and tiny dancing embers that swirled around her head like a crimson snowstorm, but the night was cold: a bitter wind cut through her parka and whipped her hair around her face. The streets ran with water from the firemen's hoses, reflecting the orange light of the flames and soaking through Rose's boots.

'Get back!'

There were vehicles everywhere, and noise, men with

pumps and hoses, black against the smoke, directing long streams of water up, up, up, into the heart of the fires. Nobody seemed to notice the two girls and the dog amidst the rattle of the pumps, the roar of the flames and the ever-present thrum of the planes overhead.

Where are you? Where are you?

'Take cover!'

The men threw themselves on to the road as a bomb screamed down and exploded with a bone-juddering thud. Rose turned her face to the sky and thought of the men in the plane. She couldn't see the moon any more, or the stars. They had been blotted out by smoke.

'Over here, mate! Here!'

And still the planes kept coming, dropping their incendiary bombs in showers to clatter like rain on the pavements and roofs around the square and hiss into life like poisonous fiery snakes. The burning buildings cracked and groaned as if their bones were breaking, and always there was the joyful cruel roar of the flames.

'Rose!' Rosemary clutched her hand so tightly it hurt.

Two men had appeared like ghosts out of the smoke. One was injured, supported by his friend. Their faces were blackened by the smoke, just their eyes showed white, they could've been anybody. But neither of them was Johnny. Rose felt Rosemary's hand go limp with disappointment.

Where is he? Where is he? *Where is Johnny?*

And then, through the smoke she saw them. Two firefighters, manhandling a hose between them, directing the line of white water against the wall of one of the buildings in a side street. The water was blowing back towards them, the men were soaked, their faces streaming as they battled with the hose, using all their strength to keep themselves upright, to keep the water flowing towards the pulsing heart of the fire. One of them was tall, slim . . .

And then he turned towards them and she saw his face.

And it wasn't Johnny.

All the men looked the same, with their helmets and their overalls, their boots and their blackened faces, streaked with sweat or water or both, their voices croaking orders to each other as they worked the pumps and heaved the great lengths of hose, directing the water at the burning buildings. It was as if they were part of the fire, as if it was some huge furnace that needed to be kept alight, that they were working to feed, instead of trying to put it out.

I can't see. I can't see, Tommy!

He was beside them, close enough to touch, Rose could feel his body against her leg. But the smoke was so thick and her eyes burned. She thought she saw the moon through the smoke but it was just the huge clock face on the tower of Big Ben, glowing orange in the reflected light. As she looked, trying to make out the time, it started to chime.

The familiar notes sounded strange amidst the rattle of the pumps and the roar of the flames and the thrum of the bombers' engines. How come it was still working in the middle of all this, when everything else was broken? Was that why it was covered in scaffolding?

The big bell started to strike the hour.

There were four bongs, Rose counted them. So it was morning. A new day had begun and still the fires burned on. And still they hadn't found Johnny.

Where is he? hummed the planes. *Where is he? Where's Johnny?*

'Take cover!'

The men threw themselves on to the road as another high-explosive bomb screamed down. It was close, this time, very close. When Rose opened her eyes, the men were struggling to their feet, weary but determined to battle on. And then she saw the looks of horror on their faces as they realised that this bomb had found its mark. It had gone through the roof of the building they had come to protect. It had hit the Houses of Parliament.

'All hands!'

'All hands!'

'All hands to Old Palace Yard!'

The men's boots pounded on the paving stones as they ran past, heaving hoses, manhandling pumps, shouting their desperate instructions. Smoke was already pouring out of the gaping hole in the roof and flames were creeping along the gutters. And then Rose saw something else.

'*Rosemary!*'

High up on the scaffolding that surrounded the tower of Big Ben was a lurid white light, fizzing and crackling away like an evil firework. An incendiary bomb had landed on the wooden scaffolding just below the face of the clock. The fire hadn't got hold yet, but when it did, Rose knew that London's best-loved landmark would go up in smoke.

'Someone's got to climb up there and put it out!' she yelled. 'If they don't—'

She stopped. Rosemary was staring up at the tower, her lips slightly apart. Climbing up the scaffolding, battling against the wind, was a tall, slim figure in the overalls and helmet of a fireman. There was no mistake this time. It was Johnny.

'*Johnny!*'

Although he couldn't have heard Rosemary's voice, Johnny paused for a second and looked down. Some of the men, rescue workers and others who weren't battling the fires, had spotted him too and called their encouragement.

'That's it, mate! Keep going!'

'You're nearly there, pal!'

He climbed on, through the smoke and the snowstorm of burning embers, up towards the clock face. A gasp went up from watchers below and Rose felt her friend's fingernails dig into the back of her hand as his foot on the ladder slipped. But he held firm and climbed on, up, up, up, until at last he was there. The bomb was just a few yards away, spitting its deadly white fire into the darkness. Johnny pulled himself upright on to the wooden platform and then slowly turned his head to look at the bomb, as if it was someone he didn't much like who had unexpectedly called his name.

Rose held her breath as Johnny started to move towards the bomb, putting one foot down in front of the other as if he was afraid a sudden movement would scare it away.

Easy does it now, easy . . .

He stopped a few feet away and seemed to gather himself together, then in one slow movement, removed his helmet and lobbed it gently over the sparkling white light as if he was throwing a Frisbee in the park. A cheer went up as the light went out.

'YES!'

The two men nearest Rose hugged each other and did a little dance of glee as if their favourite football team had just scored a goal. She turned to look at Rosemary. He'd done it! Johnny had saved the tower of Big Ben!

Rosemary wasn't there.

Rose hadn't seen her go. She hadn't even noticed her let go of her hand.

'Rosemary?'

Where was she? Where had she gone?

'Rosemary!'

Rose felt Tommy's body vibrate with a small worried growl. Across the road from the clock tower, along the Victoria Embankment, the main road that ran alongside the river, there were tall buildings, four or five storeys high, all ablaze. There were flames dancing out of their windows and smoke pouring from the roofs. And standing right in front of them, silhouetted against the glow, was Rosemary. She must've gone there to get a better view, to see Johnny save Big Ben. But now–

'*ROSEMARY!*'

It was no good. She couldn't hear anything above the roar of the flames.

'Tommy. Stay.'

He wagged his tail once to show he understood and sat down on the wet pavement. Rose stepped into the street. A blast of heat blew in her face as she approached the burning building and a thousand tiny red sparks swirled around her. She looked back. Tommy was there, the tower of Big Ben behind him, his white fur pink in the firelight. Ahead of her was Rosemary and the fire, breathing rhythmically like some living creature.

And then, a voice came through the smoke behind her.

'Rosemary!'

It was a voice Rose knew. A warm voice with some sort of accent . . .

'Get back! The wall's going to go!'

It was Johnny. He must have reached the ground safely. But what did he mean, the wall was going to go?

'*Get back!*'

The building groaned like an old man getting up from a chair.

'*ROSEMARY!*'

She heard him at last and turned, her face softening

into a smile as she saw him through the smoke. Beyond her, the wall bulged as if some giant hand was pushing it gently from behind. Rose felt a rush of air as Johnny ran past and for a moment he and Rosemary just stood there, close together but not touching, looking at each other, just like they had at the end of the dance on New Year's Eve.

There was a long rattling crack from the building. Rosemary and Johnny wrapped their arms around each other and turned to look at the wall. Everything stopped. Time froze solid and Rose thought of nothing at all.

And then the wall came down.

18

'What are the chances, eh?' The man nearest Rose was wearing the tin helmet of a rescue worker and his mouth was hanging open in disbelief. 'What are the blinking chances?'

Rose had shut her eyes when the wall came down, not wanting to see what happened to Rosemary and Johnny, not wanting to see anything at all. The entire world seemed to rock around her as the wall crashed into the street. And then, as the seconds slid past and the noise died down, she'd heard the rescue worker's voice above the rattle of the pumps and the roar of the flames.

'I don't believe it!'

So she'd opened her eyes. And they were still there.

Rosemary and Johnny were still standing there, wrapped in each other's arms as the dust and smoke rose up around them and the fires roared behind them, sending their flames up towards the sky.

How could that be? How was it possible?

Then Tommy barked and someone yelled and everything started to move. Rose was the first to get to them. She stumbled through the rubble and put her arms round both of them, unable to speak, to think, to breathe. There was blood on Johnny's face and Rosemary was shaking and crying and laughing, but they were safe. They were safe, safe, safe.

And now they were all in an ambulance with the same rescue worker, driving back over Westminster Bridge, leaving the fires behind them. Big Ben had been saved and the firemen had managed to contain the fire in the Houses of Parliament. It was over.

The rescue worker shook his head and called forward to the driver, still unable to believe what he had seen.

'I said, what are the chances? Whole front wall of the building come down around them and they just stood there! Just stood there, didn't they, in the gap where one of the windows had been.'

Johnny was on a stretcher with Rose's parka over him. His eyes were closed and Rosemary was crouching beside him on the floor of the ambulance, holding his hand.

'It was like that bloke in the silent movies, what's his name? Comedian. Sad face. You know the one.'

'Buster Keaton.' The driver swung the vehicle off the road. 'Buster Keaton, that's him. I don't know. What are the chances, eh?'

The ambulance stopped and the driver got out, slamming the door behind him.

'Here we are, my darlings. Told you it wasn't far.' The rescue worker jumped out as the driver opened the back doors.

'Is he your young man, love?' he said, looking at Rosemary.

Rosemary's face was black from the smoke and streaked with water, but her eyes were shining, whether with tears or happiness, Rose couldn't tell. She nodded. 'Yes. Yes, he is.' Then, 'He is going to be all right?'

'He is, darling. Thanks to you.' The two men manoeuvred Johnny's stretcher out of the back of the ambulance. 'Whatever made you think of it? Staying upright like that? Standing there like statues while a hundred ton of hot bricks fell down around you?'

Rosemary shook her head. 'I don't know.'

'It was a blinking miracle, that's what it was. A blinking miracle.'

Rose had clambered out of the ambulance and was looking at the sky. A greenish dawn was beginning to break through the haze that hung over the ruined city, and as she watched the seagulls drifting over the river, a long blast of sound came shimmering across the water. It wasn't like the horrible wailing moan of the air raid warning. It was one constant note that sounded defiant and reassuring. Safe.

'That's the all-clear.' The men had paused to listen too, holding Johnny between them, still unconscious on his stretcher. 'It's over for tonight at least.' The rescue worker looked at Rose. 'Do you not want your coat, love?' He looked down at her parka. She'd put it over Johnny after they'd helped him away from the fallen wall. He'd been soaked through with water from the hose and she didn't want him to get cold. 'It's got blood on it, I'm afraid.'

'No, I'll be all right.' Even though the sun was struggling to get through the smoky haze, it felt like the day was going to be a good one. 'What's the date, by the way?' she said. 'I've sort of lost track of time.'

'The date? It'd be, now let me think, the tenth, no I tell a lie, it's the eleventh now, the eleventh of May. 1941!' he added and grinned.

The eleventh of May. It was Mum's wedding day. And Rose needed to be there. She wanted to be there, actually, to tell her mum that she was right to hold on to her new love. And that she, Rose, was happy for her.

'The beginning of the end of the beginning, that's what I reckon,' said the rescue worker. 'It can't get any worse than last night, that's for sure. What do you think, Joe?'

The driver shrugged and jerked his head towards the hospital entrance. It was St Thomas's, the one where Rose had looked for Betty on that awful New Year's Day that was yesterday and five months ago. Their ambulance was one of many waiting to deliver patients. Nurses were bustling about in the chilly morning light, helping those people who could walk, checking those that were being brought in on stretchers.

'Rosemary?' Rose looked over at the girl who was to become her aunt and had become her friend. Maybe the best friend she'd ever had. 'What do you want to do?'

Rosemary didn't reply. She was looking down at Johnny.

'Hello,' she said.

He'd opened his eyes. A slow smile spread over his face as his eyes focused on her.

'Hello, you.'

The two men holding the stretcher exchanged a look. One grinned, the other rolled his eyes. But they didn't move.

Rosemary smiled back at the face on the stretcher. 'They say you're going to be all right.'

'That's good.' He sounded sleepy. Then, as if he'd just remembered, 'I'm leaving tomorrow.'

Rosemary didn't move. 'What?'

'My commission came through.'

141

'The RAF?'

He nodded, grimacing a bit with pain. 'Going to a place called Padgate for basic training.'

'And then?'

'Who knows?'

''Scuse me, love.' It was the rescue worker. 'Much as I hate to interrupt, my arms are killing me. And we best take him in.'

'Can I go with him?'

He shook his head. 'Against the rules, I'm afraid. The hospital's that busy. But he'll be all right.'

'Yes. Yes,' she said, then looked down at Johnny. 'I'll see you again, though?'

'You will,' he said. 'I promise.'

There was a pause. The stretcher-bearers exchanged another look.

'Well, go on then,' said the first.

Rosemary looked at him. 'What?'

'Give him a kiss. Then we can all get out of the road and on with our blooming day.'

Rosemary looked over at Rose and Tommy. Rose mouthed, 'Go on!' and Rosemary grinned, her teeth very white in her smoke-blackened face, then bent down and kissed Johnny on the mouth, before straightening up.

'Right then,' said the rescue worker. 'Let's get a move on!'

But as they started to move, Johnny stopped them.

'Wait!' He was holding something out to Rosemary. She took it and clutched it tightly in her fist as they carried him away.

Rosemary stood there for a moment, her back stiff, then turned. She looked lost and confused, as if she was a little girl who'd lost her mum in a crowd. When her eyes found Rose, she looked relieved for a second and then her face crumpled.

Rose opened her arms and, for the second time that night, Rosemary walked into them. Rose didn't know how long they stood there, locked together like Rosemary and Johnny had been when the wall came down, and when they eventually separated, she didn't know if the wet on her face was Rosemary's tears or her own. They looked at each other and then laughed as they realised they both looked as mad as each other, with their faces blackened with smoke and smeared with tears.

'What did he give you?' said Rose.

Rosemary unfurled her fist. Inside was the gold signet ring Rose had seen in Aunt Cosy's memory box.

'It's too big,' she said, twirling it on her thumb. 'But I'll keep it for ever.'

Rose nodded. 'What will you do now?'

Rosemary shrugged. 'Wait here. See if they'll let me see him before he has to go.'

'And if they don't?'

'I'll keep waiting. He'll come back and find me. I know he will.'

Rose said nothing. Rosemary looked so happy, so sure of herself and her love. She couldn't tell her that Johnny wasn't going to be able to come back and find her – that he'd go off to join the RAF and be sent on a mission and get shot down over Europe. That she'd never see him again. So she just smiled back into those shining dark eyes and turned to look out over the river. The tide was out and an old woman was down on the mud feeding the seagulls. She was wearing what looked like a blue dressing gown and red slippers, and when Rose waved she blew her a kiss from the tip of one finger.

'It's her again.' Rosemary was looking at her too. 'Is it you she's following? Or me?'

'Both of us, I think,' said Rose.

'But what's she doing here? What does she want?'

Rose took a deep breath. 'I think she wants me to be part of her memories,' she said. 'So whatever happens, today, tomorrow, or seventy-five years from now, they won't ever be lost.'

'I don't understand.'

'I'm not sure I do, completely. But I do know one thing. It's time for me to go home now.'

Rosemary nodded. She seemed to know that Rose didn't really belong here and that whatever it was she'd come to do was over. 'I couldn't have gone through this without you, Strange Girl. Will I ever see you again?'

Rose looked at her. 'Oh yes,' she said. 'You'll see me again. I can promise you that.'

19

The nearest underground station was Waterloo, but the streets around it had been cordoned off, so Rose and Tommy carried on walking until they got to Elephant and Castle. The lifts weren't working and there were no escalators at this station, so Rose led the way down the gloomy spiral staircase, stepping over people who had bedded down on the steps and were slumped against the walls, wrapped up in blankets and overcoats. Rose wondered how they could sleep, it looked so uncomfortable. But at least they were safe from the bombs.

There were more sleeping people at the bottom, rolled up in their bedding, with their sad bundles and tatty little suitcases beside them. One woman, wrapped in a faded patchwork coverlet, lay with her children lined up next to her, three on either side. Five of them were asleep, their tufty heads sticking out from under the blankets, but the sixth – a little boy of about five or six – was awake and reading a comic. He looked up as Rose and Tommy walked past and stared at them with round blue eyes.

'Hello,' he said. 'Can I pet your dog?'

Tommy was wagging his tail and sneezing with excitement. Rose nodded.

'What's his name?' said the boy as he scratched Tommy in his favourite place behind the ears.

'Tommy,' said Rose. 'What's yours?'

The boy wiped his hand on the back of his shorts and held it out for Rose to shake. It felt small and sticky in her hand. 'Brian,' he said. 'Brian Albert Henry Thompson.'

Rose's stomach flipped. It couldn't be, could it? But when she looked into the round blue eyes gazing at her from the boy's grubby face she knew they couldn't belong to anyone else.

It was her grandad.

Before she could say anything else, the ground started to tremble. A train was arriving. Rose smiled at the boy and Tommy gave one last wag before they hurried through to the platform. It was crowded with more people, waking up, yawning and grumbling, disturbed by the arrival of the first train of the morning.

'Sorry,' said Rose. It was so difficult to avoid treading on blankets, tripping over bags. 'Sorry, sorry, sorry.'

The doors slid open and they stepped on. It was a southbound train, heading for her station at Clapham South, but would it be the right Clapham South? Would it take her home?

She sat down on the prickly seat with Tommy at her feet and watched the familiar stations slide past.

Kennington, Oval, Stockwell . . .

The doors opened at every stop but no one got off and no one got on. The train was completely empty.

Clapham North, Clapham Common . . .

'Next one, Tom.'

Clapham South.

They got off. The doors closed behind them and the train drew away. Rose took a deep breath and then looked around. The platform was empty but there was an advert for a mobile phone company on the wall and an empty fried chicken box down on the track beneath the rails. There was no smell of toilets and damp clothes and unwashed people. This station had an early-morning smell of bleach and electricity. And then, an elderly black woman came through from the passage carrying a shopping bag, followed by an Indian man with a briefcase and a Chinese couple with a little girl and Rose knew.

They were home.

Outside the station, dawn was breaking over Clapham Common. The woman who owned the flower shop was pulling up the metal shutters and the early-morning bus that rumbled down Nightingale Lane looked reassuringly shiny and modern. The police cars and fire engines that had been lined up along the side of the road were gone. They must have dealt with the wartime bomb, made it safe and taken it away. The old brick shelter opposite the station was the only reminder of what had happened here all those years ago.

'Hello, Strange Girl.'

Rose knew Aunt Cosy would be there, sitting on the steps of the bandstand watching the sparrows picking up cake crumbs from the tables outside the cafe.

'We've been on quite a journey together, haven't we?' The old lady smiled at Tommy as he wagged his tail in greeting. 'We three.'

Rose nodded and sat down next to her. 'Did you ever find out what happened to him, Aunt Cosy?'

Aunt Cosy shook her head. 'My Johnny? No, sweetheart. I never saw him again, not after that night. The

Longest Night they called it, the worst night of the Blitz. It was never so bad again.'

'Do you think he was killed?'

'I don't know. When Billy showed me the piece in the newspaper, about him being missing, I feared the worst.'

'But he would've come back, wouldn't he? If he'd survived, I mean, been taken prisoner or something?'

Aunt Cosy shook her head. 'No, sweetheart. They were repatriated, you see. After the war ended.'

Rose felt a hot stab of fury. '*What?*'

'The non-Europeans, colonials as they called them. They were sent home. Back to their own countries. Johnny would've been sent back to British Guiana.'

'But that's disgusting! They came over to help and then just get sent back, like—'

Aunt Cosy patted her hand. 'It's all right, Strange Girl. I didn't really lose him. He'll always be here.' She tapped the side of her head. 'And now he's here too.' She tapped the side of Rose's head and gave one of her smiles. 'Safe. Shall we go home now?'

Mum was in the kitchen making coffee when they got back. She was wearing an old dressing gown of Dad's over her pyjamas and her hair looked mad.

'There you are!' She folded Rose into her arms. 'We were worried when we got up this morning and you weren't here. Sal said you'd probably taken Tommy out, but he's gone off to look for you anyway. Why do you smell of bonfires?' She released Rose and looked at her, holding her at arm's length. 'And why is your face all black?'

Rose rubbed her face on her sleeve and looked at Aunt Cosy for help. She didn't know what to say. How could she explain what had happened? She didn't know herself.

'We went out for a little walk, didn't we, Rose?' Aunt Cosy came to the rescue.

Mum stared, noticing for the first time that the old lady was in her dressing gown and slippers. 'Did you go out like that?'

Rose pulled a face and nodded.

'Did I?' Aunt Cosy looked down at herself. 'Oh dear! Not really dressed for a walk, am I? Or a wedding, come to that! So, if you two lovelies will excuse me . . .'

Mum waited till Aunt Cosy had sailed out before turning back to Rose. 'She's getting worse, Rose. What are we going to do?'

'I think she'll be all right now, Mum.' Rose was at the sink filling up Tom's water bowl. She put it down for him and he drank in big slurping gulps.

'What makes you think that?' said Mum.

'Oh, I don't know. Just something she said when we were out.'

'Oh good. That's good. Very good.' Mum tried to smile, but couldn't.

'Mum—' Rose stopped. Mum's face had crumpled up like a little girl's who was trying not to cry. She sank into a chair and hid her face in her hands and when Rose put a hand on her back, she felt it shaking. 'Are you OK?'

Mum took a deep shuddering breath and looked up at her. 'Yes!' she said. Then, 'No,' she said. 'Not really.' She drew an S on the table in a puddle of spilled milk.

Rose sat down next to her. 'What's up?' She touched the sleeve of her dad's dressing gown. It was an old-fashioned one, brown and red checks, a bit scratchy. It might even have belonged to Grandad once. Mum used to wear it in the months after Dad died, but she hadn't got it out for ages.

'I'm scared,' said Mum.

'Of?'

'This.' She gestured around her. 'Everything. You. Sal. Leo.' She looked at Rose. Her lip trembled. 'Your dad.'

'Oh, Mum.' Rose put her hand over her mum's hand. 'Dad's not gone away, not completely. He's still here.' She touched the side of her head, like Aunt Cosy did at the bandstand. 'And here.' She touched the side of Mum's head. 'And you getting married again isn't going to change that.'

'I know, but . . .' Mum looked at her. He eyes were wet. 'It's you, love. Are you OK with it? Because if you're not—'

'I am,' said Rose. 'I'm more than OK with it, Mum. I'm happy. Really, really happy.'

'Rose?' It was Sal. He'd come in the back door, his hair wild, his eyes worried. 'Is everything OK?'

Rose got up from her chair. 'Yes, Sal. Everything's fine.' She put her arms round him and gave him a hug, breathing in his smell of woolly jumpers and coffee and the stuff he put on his beard and wondering why on earth she'd ever thought it was weird. Then she turned to her mum.

'Come on, Mum. Let's do something about your hair.'

So Mum had got in the shower and Rose had helped her into her dress and blow-dried her hair and painted her fingernails with dark-grey nail varnish, which Mum thought was strange, but Rose knew looked stylish. Then, she and Aunt Cosy went out into the garden with Tommy and picked sprays of purple lilac from the tree near the Anderson shelter and sprigs of rosemary from the bush by the back door because Aunt Cosy said it was lucky. And at the last minute Rose had rushed into the shelter and grabbed the lipstick from the memory box, and

Johnny's ring.

And now she was in her room. Her phone was charging by the bed and she'd had her shower and put on the purpley-blue dress that had been waiting for her behind the door. Her bridesmaid's dress.

'What do you think, Tom?' He had a sprig of lilac stuck in his collar for his role as official bridesdog and was looking important and embarrassed at the same time. Rose looked back at her reflection. 'It needs something.'

Her eyes rested on the little gold lipstick on her desk. But before she could pick it up, her phone buzzed.

It was Fred, a message from last night that had only just come through.

Too late rose, it said. *I'm on way to airport see you tomorrow like it or not hahaha x*

And Rose replied:

I do like it fred sorry for before I was stupid xxx

As she pressed send there was a tap at the door.

'Cabbage?'

Grandad was wearing what he called his 'one good suit' which made him look like somebody else.

'Oops,' he said, pretending to back out. 'I'm so sorry, madam. I seem to have got the wrong room. I was looking for my granddaughter. She's a scruffy little oik who never combs her hair, not an elegant young lady such as yourself—'

Rose hugged him to shut him up. 'Grandad, I'm so, so, sorry. About Fred, I mean.'

He drew back to look at her. '*You* are?' he said. 'It's me that should be sorry. I should never have—'

'Well, he's coming anyway, so you can shut up and take Tommy for me.'

'Is he now? Well well well!' He clipped on Tommy's lead and laughed. 'Is he indeed?'

'Brian!' Rose pointed to the door.

'All right, all right, I'll say no more. Come on, Tommo, looks like we're not wanted, mate.'

When the door was shut behind them, Rose picked up the lipstick and turned to the mirror. How did Rosemary put it on without smudging? It wasn't as easy as it looked, but after a few attempts, Rose got it right. She stood back and looked at herself in the full-length mirror.

She was perfect.

And then it was over. Promises had been made, papers had been signed and Sal and Mum were officially husband and wife. Tommy had been good, Leo hadn't lost the rings (he was his dad's best man) and Grandad had been put in charge of Aunt Cosy and had sat beside her during the ceremony and made her laugh. Fred hadn't arrived, but Rose wasn't too worried. She knew there'd be a good reason. She knew he'd get there when he could.

They were at the reception now and Rose was sitting between Grandad and Aunt Cosy. The meal had been eaten, the speeches were over (Mum's had been particularly funny even though her hair had gone back to looking mad, in spite of Rose's best efforts with the hairdryer) and the dancing was about to begin.

'It's good to see your mum so happy, isn't it?' said Grandad. His tie was crooked and the white rose in his buttonhole was looking a bit droopy. 'Sal's a lovely bloke, you know. I think your dad would have approved.'

Rose nodded and looked across at Mum. She was talking to Sal, looking very serious and tapping him on the back of the hand to make her point. He was trying hard to listen, but then suddenly kissed her on the end of her nose. She looked cross for a minute and then burst out laughing and kissed him back.

Rose smiled. 'Yes,' she said. 'It is. I'm really glad.' She was too. 'Oh, Aunt Cosy, I nearly forgot.' She felt for the signet ring in her bag. 'I thought you should wear this. As it's a special day.'

Aunt Cosy looked at the ring in Rose's hand, her face soft with memories. 'But, sweetheart, I told you. It's too big for me.'

Rose took off the chain round her neck, the one that Mum and Dad had given her all those Christmases ago, and threaded the ring on to it, then fastened it round her aunt's neck.

'What's this, Cose?' Grandad twinkled at her. 'A lover's token?'

Before Aunt Cosy could reply, there was a ripple of sound from the stage as the band appeared. A buzz of expectation went through the crowd as they played a few tentative chords.

'Oi-oi,' said Grandad to no one in particular. 'Heads up, people, dancing's about to start. First dance for the happy couple!'

Rose could see Sal looking across at Mum, but she was doubled up laughing with her friends and hadn't noticed that she was expected to take to the dance floor with her new husband.

'Best go and have a word, pet,' said Grandad. 'Your mum seems to have lost the plot.'

Rose nodded and was just about to get up when she realised that Sal was onstage, tapping the microphone.

'Ladies and gentlemen!' he said. 'Can I have your attention, please?'

The laughter and chatter faded.

'Before we all take to the dance floor, I want to thank you all for coming and introduce a special guest.' Sal looked at Mum and grinned. This was clearly a surprise that he'd been planning. 'Many of you have known this lady far longer than I have,' Sal went on. 'But in the short time since she welcomed me and Leo into her home, I've come to love and respect her as much as I know you do.'

Rose looked at Aunt Cosy. She had taken her hat off and was sitting very upright, her eyes fixed on Sal as if she knew exactly what was coming.

'What I've only recently found out, however, is what a wonderful singer she is. So please, will you welcome to the stage, our lovely Miss Rosemary Miles!'

Aunt Cosy didn't need to look at Rose for reassurance this time. There was applause and some cheers as she got to her feet and made her way to the stage. Sal bent to kiss her on the cheek before leaving her alone with the musicians. And then she began to sing.

'*I'll be seeing you, in all the old familiar places . . .*'

The pianist picked up the melody, just like at Covent Garden.

'*That this heart of mine embraces . . .*'

The rest of the band followed as she sang on.

'*All day through . . .*'

Grandad took Rose's hand. She saw tears glistening in his eyes. Dad had always said he was a sentimental old fool.

'*I'll find you in the morning sun . . .*'

Rose felt the air in the room change as Aunt Cosy faltered. Just like before, the musicians exchanged glances and the pianist played a ripple of notes. The old lady was standing quite still, looking over the heads of the people sitting at the tables, towards the door. Rose was afraid to follow her gaze. But she did.

And there he was.

Standing in the doorway, transfixed by the electric

beam of Aunt Cosy's gaze, was an old man in a grey suit. His hair was white but he was still upright, still slim, still handsome. And in his hand was a dirty, crumpled white card with faded gold writing . . .

The invitation Rose had left in the pocket of her parka seventy-five years ago:

WE'RE GETTING MARRIED!
Please join Elizabeth, Sal,
Rose, Leo, Rosemary and Tommy
at 2.00 p.m. on 11th May 2016
at the Windmill Inn, Clapham Common
to celebrate our wedding!

It couldn't be. It *couldn't* be. But it was.

It was Johnny. He had survived after all. And now he'd come back to London to find his long-lost love.

People were murmuring to each other and shaking their heads. They could tell something was happening but they didn't know what. Grace was looking across at Rose, pulling a 'what the . . . ?!' face.

'*I'll find you in the morning sun . . .*'

Aunt Cosy was singing again. But not as Aunt Cosy.

'*And when the night is new . . .*'

She was the young girl again, in her scarlet dress, singing to the boy she loved. She was Rosemary.

'*I'll be looking at the moon . . .*'

'Who is that, Cabbage?' said Grandad in Rose's ear. 'Do we know him?'

'It's Johnny,' said Rose. 'His name's Johnny.'

'*But I'll be seeing you . . .*'

Aunt Cosy had come down from the stage and was making her way through the tables to the doorway. She took Johnny's hand and led him on to the dance floor.

Grandad was looking over at the door again. 'Oi-oi,' he said. 'Looks like we've got another late arrival.'

Rose felt Tommy's tail thumping against the floor from his place under the table at her feet as Grandad nudged her. Fred was standing in the doorway.

'I knew he'd come,' said Rose. She watched him for a minute as he scanned the room, looking for her, pushing his fair hair out of his eyes with one hand. And, just like she did at the dance at Covent Garden all those years ago, she thought:

I'm happy. I, Rose, am happy.

And then Fred saw her and his face lit up into a smile as he made his way over and Rose's happiness was complete.

'I am sorry to have arrived so late,' Fred said in his careful English. 'My flight was delayed. I hope I have not missed too much?'

'Nothing important,' said Rose. 'Shall we dance?'

About Rose
in the Blitz

Like most stories, *Rose in the Blitz* is a mixture of things that happened and things that are made up; places where I've been and places I've only heard about; people I've known and people I've only met in dreams . . .

And I think that's what our memories are like too. We remember the important bits, the meaningful things, the times that were particularly happy or scary or sad; but we also remember smells and feelings and sights and sounds that don't seem to have any particular meaning and sometimes might not even have happened at all. Sunny days in photographs and scary first days at school our parents told us about; the smell of our grandma's house or a pet rabbit's clean fur; the sound of seagulls or the feel of our best friend's hand . . .

You might have noticed that this book is dedicated to the memory of my mum and dad. They both died, as very old people, in 2014, the year I finished writing my other book about Rose and Tommy (it was called *Valentine Joe*). You might also have noticed that, like the characters in this book, my mum was called Rosemary and my dad, John (though he was always known as Jack).

That doesn't mean my mum and dad were the Rosemary and Johnny in this book. Mum had trained as an actress and, like Rose's 'aunt', she was known as Cosy in the family and was a bit of a show-off. Like Aunt Cosy, she also owned a Chinese jacket made of black silk and embroidered with birds and flowers and dragons that she brought out for special occasions (I've got it now). But she was only eleven when the Second World War broke out and she didn't live in Nightingale Lane, Clapham. She lived in Worthing. Like Johnny, my dad joined the RAF at the age of nineteen. His plane was also shot down over Europe and he ended up in a prisoner of war camp. But he didn't come from British Guiana (it's called Guyana now and isn't British any more). He came from Ipswich. He survived his time in the POW camp and, when the war was over, he was brought home, where a few years later he met the girl who was to become my mum.

Like many men who'd been through either of the two World Wars, my dad never talked about his experiences (partly because I think he felt it would be showing off), but Mum did. She loved to tell us about keeping chickens in the garden and the shortage of sweets and always hoping that the air raid warning would go off during Maths so you could go down to the shelter and sing songs instead of doing sums; about her dad being away and her brother being in the Home Guard and being woken up in the middle of the night by a loud bang and her mum saying, 'Go back to sleep, dear, it's only a bomb.'; about being evacuated to a family with a big house in Yorkshire where there were ponies and servants and you had to say prayers before breakfast; about soldiers everywhere (she always thought how boring life would be without soldiers!) and seeing the Emperor of Ethiopia walking along the promenade at Worthing with his family, and barbed wire on the beach and girls being allowed to wear trousers; and then, on the day that the war officially ended, going up to London with her mum on the train and dancing in Trafalgar Square and spending the night on a bench in St James's Park because they'd missed the last train back to Worthing . . .

All my mum's memories became part of my own memory and my life. They still are. So, when Mum got really old and, like Aunt Cosy, started to show signs of memory loss, I wanted to try and make sure they would never be forgotten. But I wasn't sure how to do it.

And then something else happened. Mum started to see things that weren't there. It's not particularly unusual for people with memory loss and can sometimes be quite scary. It wasn't with Mum, though. She used to see two little boys out of the corner of her eye who would follow her around and appear at inconvenient moments when she was in the Co-op or having her eyes tested. I got intrigued by these little boys and used to ask her about them, and then started to wonder what it would be like if I could see them too. If I could see what my mum was seeing, I thought, then maybe I could really be part of her memories and share the things that had been most important to her throughout her life, before they were lost for ever.

I didn't manage it with my mum, so I decided to do it with Rose. I sent her down the escalator after Aunt Cosy into the London of her memory, the London of the wartime Blitz when, for nine months, the city was subjected to nearly nightly bombing raids.

There are three big events in the story that really did happen:

On 7 September 1940, at about five o'clock on a sunny Saturday afternoon, the people of London stopped and stared at the sky as over three hundred German bombers, escorted by over six hundred fighter planes (there to protect the bombers if they were attacked by the British planes), flew over the city to drop their bombs on the docks, factories and warehouses of the East End. The homes of many ordinary people were also destroyed and many hundreds of men, women and children were killed and injured. It was the first big raid of what became known as the Blitz.

On 14 October 1940, at about eight o'clock in the evening, a high-explosive bomb hit the road above the underground station in Balham, South London. It went through the water main and the sewer which flooded the station where the local people were sheltering, believing that they would be safe. Over sixty people were killed, although over three hundred were led to safety. There's a famous photograph that you can find online of a London bus that fell into the crater.

The night of 10/11 May 1941 became known as the Longest Night. It was the last night of the Blitz (even though London and other cities did continue to suffer raids, it was never quite so bad again) and was generally remembered as the worst. From the time of the first air raid warning at half past eleven on the night of Saturday 11 May, until the all-clear sounded at ten to six on the Sunday morning, nearly fifteen hundred people had been killed and eleven thousand buildings hit, including the Houses of Parliament. An incendiary bomb (the kind that set buildings on fire rather than blew them up) did land on the scaffolding that was covering Victoria Tower (the tower of Big Ben was hit later) and someone did climb up to put it out before the tower went up in smoke. I hope the brave police officer (I don't know his name) who was really responsible for saving one of London's best-loved landmarks, wouldn't mind if he knew that I let Johnny do it instead!

I don't know if there was a New Year's Eve dance at Covent Garden in 1940 (though the Opera House was used for dances during the war) or an unexploded bomb on Clapham Common. But I do know that there were many thousands of men (and some women) like Johnny who made their way to Britain from places like British Guiana, the Caribbean and West Africa, to join the fight against Nazism and I wanted to find a way to remember their contribution.

I wanted to find a way of remembering it all, actually.

And now I hope that you'll remember some of it too.

Rebecca Stevens
Brighton, 2016

Pages 94, 154 and 155: from 'I'll Be Seeing You',
lyrics by Irving Kahal,
music by Sammy Fain (BMG, 1938).

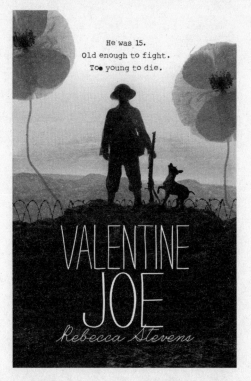

He was 15.
Old enough to fight.
Too young to die.

VALENTINE
JOE
Rebecca Stevens

VALENTINE JOE by REBECCA STEVENS

Rose goes to Ypres in Belgium to visit the graves of those who died in the Great War. There, the name of one boy stays in her mind: fifteen-year-old Valentine Joe. That night, Rose hears marching and when she looks out of her window, she sees a young soldier . . .

'A thought-provoking, original and deeply moving story which brings the war vividly to life.'
JULIA ECCLESHARE

Paperback, ISBN 978-1-909489-60-8, £6.99 • ebook, ISBN 978-1-909489-61-5, £6.99

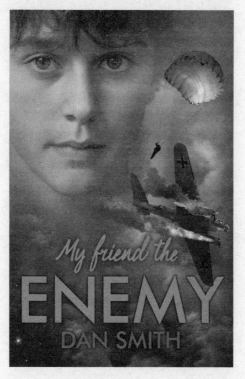

MY FRIEND THE ENEMY by DAN SMITH

1941. It's wartime and when a German plane crashes in flames near Peter's home, he rushes over hoping to find something exciting to keep.

But what he finds instead is an injured young airman. He needs help, but can either of them trust the enemy?

'. . . an exciting, thought-provoking book.'
THE BOOKSELLER

Paperback, ISBN 978-1-908435-81-1, £6.99 • ebook, ISBN 978-1-909489-06-6, £6.99

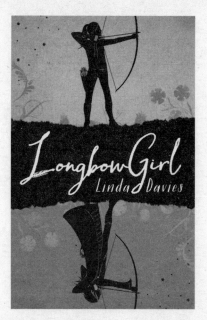

LONGBOW GIRL by LINDA DAVIES

Schoolgirl Merry faces the loss of her family's farm. For centuries, the Owens have bred ponies in the shadow of the Black Castle, the wild Welsh home of their arch-enemies, the de Courcys.

In the roots of a storm-turned tree, she makes an extraordinary discovery: a treasure that offers her the chance to turn back time and change a past filled with untold secrets and danger.

Merry is brave enough for most things. She's a skilled rider and archer: a born fighter. But is she ready for this, the greatest adventure of her life?

'Davies' love of history and folklore shine through this exciting and gripping tale of a resourceful, brave, and complex girl.'

KIRKUS

Paperback, ISBN 978-1-910002-61-2, £6.99 • ebook, ISBN 978-1-910002-62-9, £6.99